P9-BAU-795

AN IRISH CHRISTMAS

MELODY CARLSON

Grand Rapids, Michigan

Published by Fleming H. Revell
a division of Baker Publishing Group
P.O. Box 6287, Grand Rapids, MI 49516-6287
www.revellbooks.com

Printed in the United States of America

Library of Congress Cataloging-in-Publication Data

Carlson, Melody.
An Irish Christmas / Melody Carlson.
p. cm.
ISBN 10: 0-8007-1880-1 (cloth)
ISBN 978-0-8007-1880-0 (cloth)
1. Ireland—Fiction. 2. Christmas stories. I. Title.
PS3553.A73257I75 2007
813′.54—dc22 2007015221

This book is a work of fiction. Names, characters, places, and incidents are the product of the author's imagination or are used fictitiously. Any resemblance to actual events, locales, or persons, living or dead, is coincidental.

To my son Lucas Andrew . . .
whose piano skills inspired the idea
for this story while we were touring
in Ireland a few years ago.

Love,
Mom

1

Colleen May Frederick

Spring of 1963

I felt certain I was losing my son. Or perhaps I'd already lost him and just hadn't noticed. So many things had slipped my attention this past year, ever since Hal's death. But lately it seemed I was losing everything. Not just those insignificant items like my car keys, which I eventually found in the deep freeze beneath a carton of Green Giant mixed vegetables, or my favorite pair of calfskin gloves, which I still hadn't located. But it seemed I was losing important things as well. Or maybe I was just losing my grip.

I studied the piles of financial papers that I had neatly arranged across the surface of Hal's old rolltop desk, the one his grandfather had had before him. I restraightened my already tidy stacks of unpaid bills, insurance papers, and miscellaneous mishmash, hoping that would help create a sense of order from what felt more like chaos. But I was still overwhelmed. So much I didn't understand. So much that Hal had handled, always somewhat mysteriously—or mysteriously to me.

Oh, I could run a household like clockwork. And I even helped out at the shoe store when needed, as long as it didn't involve keeping the books or ordering merchandise or anything terribly technical. The truth was, other than helping customers find the right shoes, ringing up sales, smiling, chatting, inquiring about an aging grandmother or a child who'd had a reaction to a vaccination, I was not terribly useful. And more and more I was feeling useless. And overwhelmed.

I hadn't heard from my son Jamie in weeks, even with college graduation right around the corner, not a word. I finally resorted to calling his dorm, but even then only received vague and unhelpful answers from a guy named Gary. I wondered what Hal would do if he were still alive. Of course, I knew what he'd say. He'd tell me not to worry so much. He'd say that I should pray instead. Easier said than done.

It had been Hal's idea that Jamie attend his alma mater, an expensive private business college in the Bay Area. And Jamie had been thrilled at the prospects of living in San Francisco, several hours away from us. He longed for independence and freedom. But after a few semesters, Jamie grew disenchanted with the small college and wanted to switch schools to Berkeley, in particular to their school of music. Jamie honestly believed that he could make it as a musician.

Naturally, this seemed perfectly ridiculous to both Hal and me. So Hal encouraged our dreamer son to stick it out and get his business degree first. Hal told Jamie that music was perfectly fine—for fun and recreation—but it would never pay the rent or put food on the table. I had to agree.

The plan was for Jamie to take over the family business eventually. Frederick's Fine Footwear was a successful and established business in our hometown of Pasadena. It was well respected and had been in Hal's family for more than sixty years. We felt that Jamie should be honored that he was next in line for the shoe throne. As it turned out, he didn't feel quite the same. Oh, I wasn't privy to all of those "father-son" discussions that year, but it seemed they had reached an agreement of sorts, and Jamie had given up the idea of Berkeley and returned to the business college.

Then, about a year ago, it came to a head once again. At the beginning of last summer, Jamie announced that he never planned to go into the shoe business at all—period—end of discussion. Well, I know this broke Hal's heart, and I secretly believe that it contributed to the heart attack that killed him in July. Of course, I never told Jamie my suspicion. Although I know that he felt guilty enough. The poor boy blamed himself for most of the summer, even giving up a summer trip to work in the shoe store to make up for things, although I know he hated being there. Still, I reassured my son that Hal's faulty heart had nothing to do with Jamie and that his Grandfather Frederick had suffered the same ailment at about the same age.

At summer's end, I had encouraged Jamie to return to college for his senior year. The most important thing seemed to be that he would complete his education and get his business degree. What he did after that would be up to him. My son had a definite stubborn streak, and I knew that no one could force him into the shoe business. Especially not me!

And so on that warm day in May, less than a year since my husband's death, I reached for the sales contract that dominated the piles of paperwork on his neatly cluttered desk. I had decided the time had come to sell the shoe store, and under these circumstances, I felt Hal would agree. Still, it was terribly hard to sign the papers. My fountain pen weighed ten pounds as I scratched my name across those lines. I wished there were another way—or that I was made of stronger stuff. But I felt so terribly overwhelmed . . . as if I were losing everything. Maybe that's why I decided that since I was losing the shoe store, I might as well sell my house too. It was far too large for me, and expensive to maintain, what with the pool and the grounds and everything. Besides, if Jamie wasn't going to be part of my life, what would be the point? Especially when it seemed that Jamie had always been the reason for everything.

I picked up the family photo that Hal faithfully kept on top of his desk—the three of us, our happy little family. Jamie was about eleven at the time, still the little boy on the brink of adolescence. Still willing to hold my hand as we walked through town together—unless he spotted a schoolmate, then he'd let go. His dark brown hair curled around his high forehead and those brilliant blue eyes just gleamed with mischief and adventure. I studied my face next to his, the high cheekbones and pixie nose framed in dark hair. I was surprised at how young I looked back then, although it was less than ten years ago, but then again I was barely thirty. That seemed so very young now.

I pulled the picture in for a closer look. Although I had been smiling, there was sadness in my eyes. Had that always been there? Did anyone else ever notice it? Hal wore his usual cheerful grin. He had just started to bald back then, and his paunch was perfect for playing Santa, which he loved to do at the shoe store during the holidays.

Setting the frame back down on the desk, I looked at the image now blurred as tears welled up in my eyes. There we all stood, smiling midgets beneath our enormous Christmas tree, oblivious to the fact that life would be vastly different ten years later. Jamie had always insisted that the gilded star on the treetop must touch the ceiling, but our home had vaulted ceilings that stretched more than fifteen feet tall. Hal never once complained about how much trouble it had been to unearth a tree that size down here in Southern California, although one year he drove six hours to get just the right tree. Consequently Jamie had never been disappointed. Spoiled a bit, perhaps, but then he'd been our only child and such a good boy. He always made us happy to be his parents, always made us proud.

Until recently anyway.

And, in all fairness, just because a grown son hadn't bothered to call his mother in several weeks, well, I supposed that didn't make him a bad boy. Just neglectful. After all, he had his own life.

2

James William Frederick (Jamie)

I'd kept a secret from my parents for a couple of years now. It had started out to be a temporary thing—a quick fix. But when Dad died unexpectedly last summer, I thought that would end my little game. I'd planned to make a clean break of it with Mom—and I figured she'd forgive me, eventually anyway. But she seemed so fragile over losing Dad, and the shoe store needed attention, and life just got busy. One thing led to another, and before I knew it, another year had passed and I still hadn't made my disclosure. And I discovered there was something about secrets . . . the longer you keep them, the bigger they grow.

My life of deception began when I dropped out of college. It had been winter term of my junior year when I decided to call it quits. My main reason for giving up had been to pursue my music—well, that combined with a slightly broken heart, something that, unlike my music, I eventually got over—or mostly. To me, music was my life (as well as a form of therapy) and I believed I could make it into my livelihood. But my dad didn't agree. He felt that music was something to play at, but selling shoes was a *real* job. And, after my futile attempt to discuss my musician's dreams with him during Christmas break of 1961, I decided to take my future into my own hands and quietly dropped out of school without bothering to mention this minor fact to either of my unsuspecting parents.

After all, I'd convinced myself, it was my life. And it hadn't helped matters that I'd missed a lot of classes as a result of getting dumped by my girlfriend that winter. The choice was pretty obvious, and I'd figure out a way to break this news to my parents . . . when the time was right. My thinking was that when my music made me rich and famous, which I felt was inevitable, the truth would be much sweeter. In the meantime, thanks to my friend the dorm manager, I continued to live on campus, and I continued to collect my parents' monthly support checks as well as their tuition payments for the classes I wasn't taking. This benefit was accompanied with a fair amount of guilt, although I did my part to justify things. And I blamed my dad for trusting me. It had been his idea from the beginning that part of growing up and becoming a man would be for me to manage my own finances during college. I was managing them, all right.

When alleviating my guilt, I would remind myself that it had never been my choice to go to that college in the first place. Sure, it had been fine for Dad, back in the Dark Ages when a guy was considered fortunate to attend college at all. But I would've preferred attending Berkeley, specifically the school of music. And so I convinced myself that my parents' financial support was "my due pay." It wasn't easy to support a fledgling band back in the early sixties, so I figured it was an investment in my future. And it was my compensation for my hard work—my work that included writing music; purchasing, maintaining, and practicing my instruments; and performing with my newly created band, Jamie and the Muskrats. Thanks to twenty-twenty hindsight, I can now admit that our band's name didn't boost our career much, but on second thought it was just the beginning of the rock and roll era, and even the Beatles had a few kinks to work out.

"Selling shoes might be your bag," I had informed my dad when I came home to visit at the beginning of last summer. I'd probably been just a little full of myself since Jamie and the Muskrats had played two high school proms in the Bay Area the previous month, and I felt certain that fame was right around the corner. "But I refuse to spend my entire life handling stinky feet and trying to cram Mrs. Flemming's puffy size 8½Ds into 7Bs." By then I'd spent enough summer "vacations" working in Frederick's Fine Footwear to know what the shoe business was really like—up close and way too personal—and I had no intention of dedicating my life to shodding the fine but smelly feet of Pasadena.

"But Frederick's has been in our family for nearly sixty years," my dad had protested. "Your grandpa started it before I was even born, and it's been my dream that you'd take it over after graduation, Jamie. That's why I wanted you to get your business degree. I expect you to follow in my *footsteps*." Then he even chuckled at his weak pun, slapping me on the back as if that was all it took to pull me into the family shoe business.

"Sorry, Pops," I told him. "But I'm just not ready to fill those shoes." When it came to bad puns, the apple didn't fall far from the tree. So it was that we went round and round for about a week that June. And Dad even laid down some tempting offers for me. And when that didn't work, he actually resorted to some slightly camouflaged threats, like cutting off my spending money, although he'd never been the sort of man to carry out such a thing. But it was all of no use. Neither of us wanted to budge and it finally became a standoff. The shoe business might be fine for Dad and my grandpa before him, but I made myself perfectly clear: Frederick's Fine Footwear would have to get by without the youngest Frederick. And so I took off on a road trip with my band—my plan was to be gone all summer.

Then Dad suffered a heart attack in early July. It was only due to Steve, our band's drummer, that I discovered this since he had called home and heard the news from his mom just one day after Dad died. Thanks to my secret dropout status along with my refusal to play the "good son" by taking over the family business, I felt overwhelmingly responsible for my father's death. Talk about a guilt trip. Of course, Mom reassured me that it wasn't my fault at all, and that Dad had been having some "serious heart trouble" for a couple of years already. Still, I felt miserable about the whole thing. Plus, I really missed Dad. I suddenly realized that we don't really know what we have until it's gone.

So here I was stuck in Pasadena and suffering from many layers of guilt, which killed any desire to return to what had turned into a fairly lackluster road trip anyway. To ease my guilt, I volunteered to fill in at the shoe store for the remainder of the summer; it was the least I could do. But then September came and Mom insisted I return to my classes. And, fed up with hot swollen feet and cranky back-to-school shoppers, I was more than happy to comply with her wishes. I told myself that I'd write her a nice long letter and confess my lie to her later on—after she'd had more time to recover from losing my dad. There seemed no sense in adding to her load just then.

"The most important thing, right now," Mom told me as she handed me clean laundry and I packed my bags, "is for you to graduate. Don't worry about a thing. I'll handle the store from here on out. You just take care of your education, Jamie. Look toward your future."

I couldn't disagree with her about that either. But I also couldn't admit that, at the moment, my education and my future was all about music—I couldn't tell her that everything I wanted to learn either involved a guitar or a piano or my transistor radio and the Top Forty. Nor did I mention that the Muskrats and I had already lined up several more promising gigs for the upcoming fall. Instead, I just kissed her good-bye and said, "See ya at Christmas."

But autumn came and went and I had to excuse myself for Christmas because Jamie and the Muskrats had several good parties to play during the holidays. Naturally, this only added to my growing accumulation of guilt. The truth was, I felt ashamed to go home and face Mom, knowing that I was living such a lie. At the same time, I wasn't man enough to tell her the truth either. Instead I sent her an expensive hand-carved jewelry box, purchased with some gig money, as if I thought I could buy her off. Then I even called her on Christmas Eve and I told her how much I missed her and how I wished I was home, which was actually the truth. She sounded sad and slightly lost—sort of how I was feeling at the time. But I promised I'd spend next Christmas with her.

Jamie and the Muskrats got a few more frat parties that winter and a couple of high school dances that spring. But, despite these opportunities, the Muskrats were not making it to the big time like I'd planned. Ed Sullivan had not called, and consequently we knew we could never make ends meet on our musicians' wages. Plus it seemed that the band's earlier enthusiasm was definitely flagging. It didn't help matters when Gordon and Bill, about to graduate, both lined up "real" jobs for the upcoming summer. The Muskrats were about to become a duet with only my drummer buddy Steve Bartowski and me, and as far as I could see, a guitarist and a drummer did not equal a band. Then within that same week, Steve, shocked to hear of his girlfriend's pregnancy and in need of "some serious dough," enlisted in the Air Force! I couldn't believe it. Jamie and the Muskrats had been reduced to *just Jamie*, and I wasn't about to take my act out solo.

"I guess I'll come home for summer after all," I told Mom on the same day that Steve dumped me for his girlfriend and the Air Force. I'd called her long-distance—as always, collect.

"Wonderful," she said in a flat voice that lacked any genuine enthusiasm and actually sounded pretty depressed, and not a bit like the cheerful little mother I'd grown up with.

"And I can work at the store for you too," I added, hoping that might cheer her up.

"Uh, *the store*?" she said in this slightly higher pitch, like all was not well with Frederick's Fine Footwear. "I'd meant to tell you, Jamie. And I actually tried to call your dorm a couple of weeks ago, but you weren't there. The thing is I, uh, I sold the store."

"Really?" Now for some reason I felt slightly blindsided by this news. "You *sold* Dad's business and you didn't tell me?"

"Well, I knew how you felt about the shoe trade, and I have to admit I was a little overwhelmed by the whole thing myself. And you've been so busy with school and with graduation coming up . . . by the way, when is graduation, Jamie? You've been so evasive this year. I hope you didn't forget to reserve some tickets. I promised your Aunt Sally that we'd both fly up there for it. We plan to stay at the Fairmont in San Francisco, live it up a little. We need something to celebrate. Perhaps we can have you and a few of your friends for dinner while we're there. Wouldn't that be fun?"

That was when I decided my best defense might be to get defensive. "I can't believe you sold Frederick's Fine Footwear, Mom." I took on a tone that was meant to sound hurt. "I mean, just like that, you go and sell a family business that's been around for generations and you don't even consult me?"

"But I thought you didn't want—"

"How could you possibly know what I want when you didn't even talk to me about it, Mom?"

"I tried to call you . . . but I haven't heard from you for so long, Jamie."

"But I was counting on coming home this summer, I was going to work in the shoe store, Mom. I thought I might even take over running it, and now what am I supposed to—"

"Oh, Jamie!" She sounded truly alarmed. "*I had no idea!* Oh, I feel so horrible. I wish I'd known. I never would've sold it if I'd known you'd changed your mind. I'm so, so sorry."

I knew I had her where I wanted her, but I suddenly felt guilty about my tactics. Even so, I knew that before long I would have a confession to make. I knew I needed to position myself. And I guess I was feeling a little desperate. "Oh, it's okay, Mom. It's not really your fault. I guess I should've called you and said something—"

"I feel so terrible. You're absolutely right, I should've asked you, Jamie. It's just that George Hanson was so interested in buying, and I felt things were going downhill so fast, it was time to reorder merchandise for the fall season, and everything just seemed so over—"

"Really, Mom, it's okay," I said soothingly. "I just wish I'd known, that's all."

She sighed loudly.

"You really should've kept me in the loop, Mom."

"I know, Jamie. I'm *so* sorry."

"So, I'll see you in a couple of weeks then?"

"For graduation?" she asked hopefully.

"No," I answered quickly. "I decided not to do the ceremony. It's all such a production—a bunch of pomp and circumstance and stifled yawns. I just want to come home, Mom. I'd hoped to come home and take over the business and—"

"Oh, dear . . ."

"But don't worry about any of that now." I paused for dramatic effect. "I'll . . . well, I'll think of something else to do with my life."

So it was that Mom's decision to sell the business helped to counter my own dilemma and, by burdening her with layers of parental guilt, I didn't have to confess my lack of graduating with the prized business degree. But after I got home, we didn't talk too much. I wasn't sure if it was because of her or because of me. Admittedly, I wanted to avoid any conversations that might force a confession. Oh, I wanted to confess. I just wasn't sure how—or more importantly, when. As a musician, I knew that timing was everything. Still, I could tell that Mom was sad and maybe even depressed. She seemed really withdrawn and she slept a lot, but that might've been the result of some of the medication she was taking. She told me that Dr. Griswold had prescribed Valium for her nerves shortly after Dad died.

"I didn't take it at first," she told me, "but then I figured maybe it would help."

Well, I couldn't tell if it had helped or not, but it sure did knock her out. Consequently there wasn't much for me to do but hang by the pool, mow the lawn occasionally, and see if any of my old friends were in town, which didn't seem to be the case.

I'd stored most of my stuff, including my music instruments and the secondhand piano I'd purchased with my "tuition" money, in an old warehouse space that had once been used for shoe-related things but hadn't been sold along with the business. By the end of summer, I found myself spending more and more time at the rundown warehouse.

I'd pulled the piano out into the open and had begun to just play for the fun of it. But unlike the tunes I'd played for the Muskrats, this sort of playing was purely for my own enjoyment and not something I felt certain I'd want people my own age to even hear. It wasn't anything like the stuff that our generation listened to nowadays. In a way it reminded me of country music, which I claim to despise, but the beat was different. I wasn't even sure how I'd explain it, or if I cared to. But I was really getting into it, and it was a good way to kill time—perhaps it was a way to postpone the inevitable and to avoid my mother. I wasn't sure how long I could hold out, and I had no plan for how I would admit that I'd squandered my tuition money as well as nearly two years of college. Mom had always been pro-education, and who knew how she would handle such news? She was already having a hard time anyway. Why add to her stress? Besides, I told myself, she was usually sleeping anyway.

As fall approached, Mom announced that she was quitting the Valium. "It makes me feel like I'm living in a cloud," she admitted. "Like I'm half dead."

"Good for you," I told her. Still, considering the fact that she was getting back on her feet, so to speak, I didn't think it was the right time to dump on her just yet.

As September ended, both Mom and I were getting pretty antsy. I even had the gall to blame her edginess on her lack of narcotics, sometimes even suggesting, "Why don't you just pop a Valium?" which made her furious.

"Why don't you just clean up after yourself?" she'd toss back at me.

I suppose I had gotten a little sloppy. But then I'd grown up having a mom to clean up after me. And when Mom started to nag me about leaving messes in the kitchen or piles of dirty clothes in the laundry room, I'd get irritated. And if I got too worked up, like I often did, Mom would start asking what I was going to do for employment now that I had graduated.

"How do you plan to use that college education?" she would ask.

"I thought I was going to run a shoe store," I'd toss back, hoping to keep her questions at bay. Then we'd really get into it. She'd point out that it had been my choice, reminding me of how I'd made myself clear to Dad. Then I would blame her for not communicating with me. It could get pretty loud sometimes. Like that muggy evening when one of our "discussions" escalated into a heated argument, and I told Mom that I thought it was high time for me to move out.

"I need a place of my own!" I shouted at her, knowing full well that the windows were open and half the neighborhood could probably hear us.

"Fine!" she shouted back.

"And there's no time like the present!" I added, almost expecting her to back down now. Despite our disagreements, I thought she liked having me around.

"Maybe that's for the best," she said with tear-filled eyes, reaching for her pocketbook. "I'll help you get into a place, and then you can get a job and support yourself, Jamie. That would probably be good for you." She wrote me a check that would cover a month's worth of rent and buy groceries and then told me "good luck."

But by late October, I was out of money, still unemployed, about to be thrown out of my apartment, and one day, while strolling through town, I discovered that Mom had put the family home up for sale.

"What's going on here?" I demanded when I saw the real estate sign planted in the front yard. Mom was raking willow leaves and looked up at me with a weary expression. Was she tired of me or just life in general?

"This place is too big for me," she said calmly. "Too hard to keep up. Plus it's too expensive to hire someone. There's the pool and the grounds and just everything. I decided to look for something smaller, perhaps a little cottage near the ocean."

I blinked at her in surprise. *Who was this woman anyway?* What had become of my mother, that small but feisty woman who could run an impeccable household and still have time to play cards with her friends or tennis at the club? It seemed like the life had been sucked right out of this woman. It occurred to me that she probably needed my help, maybe she even wanted me to move back home. Even so, I was too proud to ask if I could come back. I wanted her to ask me. Not only that, but I was too embarrassed to admit that I was still jobless. And that naturally brought up the other part of the problem. No way did I want to confess to her that I hadn't finished college or any of my other shortcomings. No, instead I just opened my big fat mouth and the escape plan I'd recently been toying with came flying out.

"Fine," I snapped at her. "Go ahead and sell the house. You make all your decisions without me anyway. But just so you know, I plan on enlisting in the Air Force. I was on my way to the recruiter's office right now. I hear they're looking for some smart guys with a college education, and I—"

"*What?*" Mom dropped her bamboo rake and her jaw in the same instant. You'd have thought I'd just told her that I was planning on chopping off my right arm or robbing a bank or something. "Are you crazy?" she demanded, the color draining from her face.

No doubt, I had her attention now. And even though my proclamation was rather half-hatched, not to mention somewhat premature, it suddenly made perfect sense to me. Joining the Air Force sounded exciting and interesting. I'd watched their exotic TV ads about seeing the world. Plus, didn't they offer three good meals a day? That was better than I'd been doing lately. Also, I'd heard they had education benefits by way of the GI bill. Maybe I could even get my degree when I finished. Plus, it would be the perfect way to delay the inevitable—confessing all to Mom.

"My buddy Steve enlisted in the Air Force last June," I told her with false confidence. "He thinks he'll be an officer. And with this business going on in Vietnam right now, I thought why shouldn't I do the same? After all, it's my patriotic duty, and President Kennedy is the one who said, *'Ask not what your country can do for you, but ask what you can do for your—'* "

"*James William Frederick!*"

"What?"

"Have you taken leave of your senses?"

"No, Mom. I'm thinking straighter than ever at the moment. And, hey, I might even become a pilot, and I could—"

"You could get yourself killed!"

"Why do you have to go and jump to that conclusion?" I asked in a surprisingly calm voice. It was fun playing the mature person for a change. "Don't you remember how Dad used to say how much he'd wanted to enlist during World War II? Every time we watched a war movie on TV, he'd get all depressed. He felt like he'd missed out on something really important, but he told me that no matter how hard he'd tried to sign up, they refused to take him."

"That's because he was *too old*!"

Well, it was no secret that my dad had been about twelve years older than Mom. But that hadn't been too old to enlist. "He told me it was because of his flat feet."

Mom blinked, then nodded. "Yes, that's right."

Flat feet or no flat feet, there was something about the way Mom had blurted out "too old" that made me wonder if their age difference had been an issue with her. Had it bothered her that he was so much older? And now he was gone and she, only forty-one and still nice looking (for a mom anyway), was all alone. I studied her more closely. Even without makeup and twigs in her hair, she was pretty. But she looked too skinny and her high cheekbones looked even higher than usual with dark shadows in the hollows of her cheeks, and dark shadows beneath her eyes. Was she okay?

"Well, what about Henry Ackley?" I demanded, pushing my sympathetic thoughts aside, at least for the time being. I had a point to make here—about the Air Force and why I should join. Henry had been Dad's most faithful employee and a proud veteran to boot. "Henry used to tell me that joining the armed forces was the best way a man could possibly serve his country."

"Henry didn't know everything!"

"What do you mean by that?" I demanded. "Henry was always telling great war stories, acting like being in the South Pacific was the greatest time of his life. And, good grief, it had to be a lot more exciting than selling pumps to old ladies, for Pete's sake. What are you talking about anyway, Mom?"

She stepped forward and looked me in the eyes. "I'm talking about a young man—a young man with a bright future and a fine education—a young man who is willing to toss everything aside just so he can run halfway around the world to shoot guns and bombs and things!"

"Whoa, Mom," I said in an almost teasing voice. "I had no idea you were anti-war. Did Dad know about this?"

Her eyes were filled with fire now and she was really fuming. She reminded me of a character in those cartoons I used to watch on Saturdays, maybe the one where Elmer Fudd got so fed up with Bugs Bunny that the steam came pouring out his nostrils and ears as he aimed a loaded shotgun at the rabbit's head. Well, my mother looked ready to blow too. But I just shrugged, picked up her fallen rake, and took over where she'd left off, scooping a big clump of leaves into her pile.

Without saying a single word, Mom turned away and stomped off toward the house. I think I actually felt the lawn vibrating with each step. And I felt pretty sure I'd missed a bullet—a mother bullet.

But when Mom came back out again, about an hour or so later and after I'd gotten all the leaves raked into one big neat pile, she informed me that I was *not* going to enlist in the Air Force, and that I was *not* going to go to Vietnam, and that I was *not* going to become a pilot. "Not until you've accompanied me to Ireland *first*," she told me in her firmest most I-mean-business–like voice.

"Ireland?" I said, thinking my mother had finally lost her blooming mind. "What on earth for?"

"Because I said so," she said with finality. "And I've already made the travel arrangements for us. We're going there in mid-December. *For Christmas.* You'll have just enough time to get your passport. And if you know what's good for you, you will not argue with your mother, young man!"

3

Colleen

"Why in the world are you going to Ireland?" my sister demanded as I refilled our coffee cups. Sally had just driven up from San Diego and we were having our second cup of coffee. I returned the chrome coffeepot to its spot by the stove, then sat back down, placing both of my palms flat on the shiny plastic surface of my kitchen table. I studied the cheerful buttercup color of the plastic laminate and pondered her question. It was a good question—one that deserved a good answer. It had been only a week since I'd announced my crazy plan to Jamie, and to be honest, I was starting to have second thoughts myself.

"Really, Colleen," she persisted as she picked up the creamer. "What makes you want to go to Ireland? And for Christmas? You don't even know anyone over there, do you?"

"No . . ." I stirred cream into my coffee.

"Not that I wouldn't love to travel too, if I were you." She let out a long sigh, looking dreamily out my kitchen window toward the bougainvillea bush. "But Ireland?"

"Jamie was talking about joining the Air Force." I said the words slowly, still trying to absorb the meaning behind his announcement.

"So?" Sally shrugged then stirred some sugar into her cup.

"So, I didn't want him to."

"Why not?" She looked evenly at me now, and I could tell I was walking on thin ice here. Especially since her husband Richard had only recently retired from a lifetime career in the Navy and their older son Larry was considering following in his dad's footsteps after high school graduation in two years. "You have something against the military, Colleen?"

"No, no, of course not." I considered my words carefully. "It's only that Jamie just graduated from college and . . ."

"First of all, what makes you so sure about that? It's not like you *saw* him graduate, did you? Has he shown you his diploma yet?"

"No, but that's not really the point."

"What *is* the point?"

"I don't want him going off to Vietnam and getting hurt."

"Why would he get hurt, Colleen? From what I hear it's mostly about peacekeeping, restoring the order. According to Richard, it should all be over before long anyway."

"But you never know . . ."

Sally frowned, then reached over and placed her hand on mine. "It's because of losing Hal, isn't it? You're worried that since you've been recently widowed, you only have Jamie left, am I right?"

I looked out the window in time to see a goldfinch lighting on a branch, then nodded. "Yes, I suppose that has something to do with it."

"But why Ireland? And if you're worried about Jamie's safety, you might want to think again. From what I've heard about that new prime minister in northern Ireland, it's not going to be the most peaceful place either before long."

"It's hard to explain . . . but I suppose I've wanted to see Ireland for a long time."

"Is it because of your name?" Sally teased. "You think that because Mom named you Colleen means you're Irish? Because I can assure you that's not the case. She just happened to like the name. If Dad had had his way, we'd all have Norwegian names like Helga or Olga or Gudrun."

I chuckled. "Can you imagine being *Gudrun*? It sounds like a bad case of indigestion. And, no, my interest in Ireland isn't related to my name. But maybe it's because of that movie . . . remember *The Quiet Man* with John Wayne and Maureen O'Hara about ten years ago? I was so taken with it. Ireland looked like such a pretty place. So romantic."

Sally seemed to consider this, then eagerly nodded. "Oh, I loved that movie too. Well, except for the part where he spanked her. *That* was uncalled for."

I laughed, then agreed.

"So, there's no talking you out of this Ireland trip then? You and Jamie won't change your minds and come down and spend Christmas with us this year?"

"No, but thanks anyway. The travel agent has it all booked and Jamie's already applied for his passport."

"And yours must still be good."

"Yes. It's been less than three years since Hal and I went to Paris."

Sally sighed. "And I'll bet you're glad you did that, aren't you? Good thing you didn't wait for your twentieth anniversary after all. Wouldn't that have been last winter?"

I nodded. "Who knew Hal would be gone by then?"

I could almost see the wheels turning in Sally's head now. Hal and I had kept quiet about our anniversary for years, and not for the first time, I could see my sister doing the mental math, calculating about how Hal and I married in February, but how Jamie was born the following July, only six months later. And, weighing in at a hefty eight pounds four ounces, he wasn't a bit premature either. Still, as usual, Sally didn't mention this slight discrepancy. I suspected she and Richard had their own secrets too. Some sleeping dogs were better left undisturbed.

"Hi, Aunt Sally," Jamie called as he slammed the kitchen door behind him.

"You're looking fit and trim." Sally nodded approvingly at his tanned and sturdy torso, still glistening with perspiration.

"He's been helping to keep the grounds up for me, cleaning the pool and cutting the lawns and whatnot." I smiled at my shirtless son as he foraged through my refrigerator. He eventually located a bottle of Pepsi and popped the lid off with the opener tucked beneath the counter. Then he nodded to us, said a polite good-bye, and headed back out.

"I noticed the real estate sign is still up," Sally said. "You still planning to sell?"

"It's been a relief having Jamie around to help, but I can't depend on him forever, and this place is really too big for me." I set down my empty cup and pressed my lips together, unsure once again about so many things.

"It's such a beautiful home, Colleen . . ." I heard the longing in her voice.

"According to Jane, my real estate lady, there's an interested party who plans on making an offer in the next week or so."

"And then what?" Sally studied me carefully as she set down her cup. "Don't tell me you plan on moving out of here before your big trip to Ireland?"

"I don't know . . . but I didn't sell the old warehouse that Hal used for the shoe business," I explained. "I suppose I could store some things there, and then sell some things. I really won't need all this furniture."

Sally frowned. "You're okay, aren't you, Colleen? The way you're talking about selling things, packing up, and all that . . . well, you remind me of an old woman who's about to call it quits. Is there anything you're not telling me? You're not sick, are you?"

I forced a tight smile and took a small sip of coffee. "No, I'm perfectly fine, Sally. I just feel overwhelmed, that's all. I want to simplify my life." I waved my hand around the big modern kitchen with its long laminated countertops, sleek white metal cabinets, and the fancy GE appliances, all those expensive things that Hal insisted I should have when we built this house back in 1950. "I really don't need all this."

Sally laughed. "I sure wish I could trade with you. My kitchen is so tiny that if all three kids and Richard are in there with me, I can barely turn around, let alone attempt to cook anything edible."

"At least it's better than what we grew up with back in Minnesota," I reminded her. "Remember Mom's old cast iron cookstove and how hot that place got in the summertime during harvest season? It was like a Swedish sauna."

"Or a steam room if we were canning." Sally nodded grimly. "I still remember how I fumed at you for leaving home after high school. I got stuck with all the cooking for the next few years."

I smirked at my younger sister. "I did my time."

"You and me both!"

We both laughed, then as usual we recalled some of the fun parts of growing up on a wheat farm in northern Minnesota, commiserating about how it felt being the only two girls in a family with six sons who all helped our dad to work the land. We exaggerated about the size of the mosquitoes and how challenging it was to have a boyfriend with all those brothers around. I even told her the story of when our oldest brother Hank found Tom Paulson kissing me in the hayloft.

"Poor Tom," I said, suppressing laughter. "After the black eye and bloody nose, that unfortunate boy never looked at me again."

"No wonder you wanted to move out to Hollywood," Sally teased. "And, you know, Colleen, I really thought you were going to make the big times too. I used to brag to all my girlfriends, telling them how you were going to be a famous movie star. I even made up some stories, pretending like you were actually getting cast in some films. I have to confess that I even told Katherine Olson that you'd gotten a small role in a movie with Clark Gable, and she believed me."

I laughed loudly now. *"She believed you?"*

"Well, we'd all seen you in the high school plays. You were the best and you were a beauty, and everyone knew it. We thought you had a real chance."

I frowned and glanced away. "Guess we were all wrong about that."

"You *could've* been a star," Sally said stubbornly. "If you hadn't given up so quickly. We were all so shocked when you wrote home and told us that you'd gotten married. Oh, sure the war was going and all, but it still took us all by surprise."

"Oh, well . . ." I sort of shrugged and tried to think of a way to change the subject.

Sally laughed now. "I suppose that's what true love does to a person."

I stood and carried my coffee cup to the sink. "Your Julie told me that she's interested in acting," I said as I rinsed my cup. "She said she plans to try out for the school play next spring. I think she'd be a good actress."

Fortunately that was all I needed to sidetrack my sister. Soon Sally was talking about Julie and how much her only daughter had matured last summer. "She gave up all her old tomboy ways, well, besides playing basketball with the boys in the driveway, I don't think that will ever end. But did I tell you that Julie's got a little boyfriend now? Not that we're letting her date yet since she's only fifteen, but it's so cute how he calls her on the phone. Richard even got her a little pink princess phone for her bedroom last week. It's so adorable."

"Julie is such a sweetheart. I'd love to see her before we go to Ireland. You know, she's the closest thing I've had to a daughter." I smiled at my sister. "I try not to feel too envious of you."

"Believe me, there are times when I'd gladly give her to you." She set her empty cup down, then just looked at me. "Tell me, sis, why didn't you and Hal have more kids? You were such good parents to Jamie, and with this great, big house, well, it just never made sense to me."

"I would've loved more," I admitted. "But Hal had an old injury . . . you know, the sort of thing that makes it impossible to conceive children."

Sally looked truly shocked at my unexpected confession, and I suddenly realized my faux pas and wondered what I could possibly say to undo my blunder. This was what came of getting too comfortable while chatting.

"Then having Jamie was a *real* miracle, wasn't it?" Sally's eyes grew wide with curiosity.

For a brief moment, I considered telling my sister the truth—the whole truth and nothing but the truth. She was, after all, my only sister as well as my closest friend. But this was a secret I had harbored and protected for so many years, and old habits are hard to break. "Uh, actually, Hal's accident happened *after* Jamie was born." I did hate to lie, but sometimes it was a necessary evil. "It happened during the holidays, years ago . . . an eight-foot shelf overloaded with boxes of shoes toppled onto him . . . nearly killed the poor man." Well, at least that was all honest. But the real truth was that the accident happened when Hal was in his early twenties, long before I ever met him.

"I never knew that," Sally said, her finely plucked brows arched high.

"Well, it's not something we ever talked about, not even privately," I admitted. "I think Hal was very embarrassed by the whole thing." Now that was totally true.

Sally nodded. "Yes, I can understand that. I'm sure Richard would be the same way. Men are just like that."

"So, I'll trust you to keep that little confidence to yourself," I said quietly. "You know, for Hal's sake . . . and Jamie's."

"Of course." Sally glanced at the kitchen clock. "Goodness, I only meant to stay for an hour or so and it's nearly noon already. I've got so much to do. Say, why don't you and Jamie come down for Thanksgiving next month? That way you can see Julie and she can ask you all sorts of acting questions. I've been telling her about her almost famous aunt."

I chuckled. "I doubt that I can tell Julie much about acting, that was so long ago and things have certainly changed since then. But I'm sure we'd both love to come for Thanksgiving. I'll check with Jamie and call you next week. Okay?"

"Perfect!"

I watched from the living room window as Sally drove away in her old blue Plymouth, the same car she'd been driving for more than a decade now. I imagined her busy family life down in San Diego, sharing a small three-bedroom bungalow with only one bath and five people—and despite wanting to be a more mature person, I flat out envied my younger sister. I think I would've traded my modern five-bedroom house, my upscale neighborhood, the inground pool, my sleek white Cadillac, my membership at the country club, and all my fancy clothes and shoes and *everything*—well, everything except my Jamie—all of it in exchange for the simple little life that my sister had been living all these years.

And feeling like that just made me sick inside. How could I be so ungrateful? How could I be so self-centered and selfish? Think of all that dear Hal had done for me, and now all I felt was regret. But not for losing him. Oh, I did feel that too, I felt it deeply. Hal had been good to me. But, no, my regret went deeper, further back. Perhaps it was a grief that I had neglected to experience at the time—a grief that would haunt me the rest of my earthly days. Or maybe Ireland would put it to rest. One could only hope.

4

Jamie

"I hear your mother put her house up for sale," Henry Ackley said as he set a shoe box at my feet.

I'd come into Frederick's Fine Footwear for a new pair of loafers, after Mom had strongly hinted that my old ones might not be fit for international travel. I'd been trying to be a bit more congenial lately, trying to show some appreciation for the fact that Mom had invited me to move back home. I'd spent the last several days pruning shrubs, edging the lawn, washing windows, and all sorts of labor-intensive projects to make the old homestead look better—the reason being that Mom's "most serious buyer" was supposed to come by for a "third walk-through" today, and she hoped the third time would really be the charm.

"That's right," I told Henry as I slid my foot into the sleek leather shoes, lined with even more smooth leather. Now, despite my previous prejudices toward the shoe-selling business in general, I had to admit, at least to myself, that new shoes really were sort of cool. They had this certain smell and texture that just made you feel good all over. These particular loafers, with a pair of bright copper pennies tucked into the slots, would look just about perfect. And, as I extended my right foot out to admire the workmanship, a small wave of regret washed over me. Why had I so easily abandoned the opportunity to run my dad's business?

Then, as I slipped my left foot into the remaining shoe, I remembered the piece of music I'd been unable to work on this past week, and I recalled how much I missed my secret piano sessions in the warehouse, and how I planned to go over there and play for a few hours later today—and perhaps one day I'd be able to confess the whole thing to my mother, somehow make her understand. So, once again, I convinced myself that selling shoes was not what I wanted to do with my life. I sighed as I stood and looked down at this pair of swell-looking shoes.

"How do they feel?" asked Henry.

I strolled around the store now, careful to stay on the dark green carpet runners that Dad had installed himself many years ago. We always got irritated if a customer ventured off the padded surface and over to the linoleum floor, even if they did want to hear the sound of the heels clicking on the hard surface. "Nice," I told Henry. "I'll take them."

Henry grinned. "I guess that means you'll *pay* for them too. Not like the old days, eh?"

I slipped off the loafers and placed them back in the box. "Nope. Times are changing."

"How about some socks to go with them?"

I grinned at Henry, ever the salesman. "Sure," I said, going over to the sock rack and removing a couple pairs of crew socks.

"White socks with brown loafers?" He actually lifted his nose in the air.

"Like I said, times are a-changing."

He shook his head. "Brown shoes need brown socks."

I just laughed and handed him the socks.

"So, your mother really is serious about selling her house?" he asked for the second time.

"Seems to be the case." I followed him up to the cash register, wondering about his sudden interest in my mother's real estate deals. "You interested in buying it?"

He sort of laughed. "Afraid it's a little too rich for my blood."

"For hers too." I opened my billfold, feeling partially surprised to see actual money in it. My mom had been paying me for helping out these past few weeks, and for the most part, I'd been saving it. Amazing how it could begin to add up when your expenses were minimal.

Then Henry cleared his throat. "Jamie, I know it's not been much over a year since your dad passed, but do you think your mom will ever be interested in, well, you know, in seeing other fellers and whatnot?" He picked up a stubby yellow pencil and fiddled with it, obviously nervous about this out-of-character inquiry.

I blinked, then stared at him, noticing how his smooth pale cheeks were starting to flush pink. Was Henry seriously interested in my mom? "I, uh, I don't know," I said. "We don't talk usually about things like that." The truth was I couldn't imagine, for the life of me, my mother going out on a date with *any* man, let alone someone like Henry.

"Well, I can understand that, Jamie." He licked the tip of his pencil. "But your mom is a fine-looking woman and a good person to boot. I expect it won't be long before fellers start coming a-calling."

I grinned at Henry. "Would you be one of those *fellers*?"

He blushed even redder now. "Well, I might just get myself in line."

I patted him on the shoulder. "I'm sure she could do worse, Henry."

He smiled as I handed him a ten. "Thanks."

I nodded, but the image of my mother with someone like Henry Ackley made my head hurt. Oh, sure, he was a nice enough guy and all, but the two of them would be like Gomer Pyle dating Audrey Hepburn. Granted, Mom was a little older than Miss Hepburn, but she had a similar kind of class and style, and somehow I just couldn't see how Henry would fit into that picture. Of course, I'd be willing to bet there'd been those who'd said the same sort of thing about my dad. But then he'd been younger back when they'd gotten married. He'd been thinner and had a full head of hair in those days. I knew this was true because I'd seen the photos.

"So, what are your plans, son?" Henry was counting out my change now and sounding a little too fatherly, in my opinion. "For the future, I mean. What's next for young Jamie Frederick?"

I sort of shrugged, then quickly told him about Mom's plan to take me to Ireland next month. To be honest, that was about as far ahead as I could see anyway.

"An Irish Christmas?" he said with curious brows. "Interesting . . ."

"Yeah, something like that." Then I winked at him. "Actually, I think this little trip might be Mom's way of trying to talk me out of joining the Air Force."

Henry's pale eyes lit up now. "The *Air Force*? Are you joining the Air Force, Jamie?"

"Maybe so."

"Well, I'll be! That's the best darn news I've heard in weeks. The *Air Force*—now wouldn't that be something. I can just imagine you up there, flying high in one of those big old jets and serving your country with pride."

I stood a little taller. "Yeah, a buddy of mine joined up last spring, and it sounds like a pretty good opportunity for guys my age."

Henry slapped me on the back. "It'd make a man out of you, son."

Okay, I probably slumped some at that comment. I suppose I like to think that because I'm twenty-one, I'm *already* a man. But then again it might just be a matter of perspective. "Thanks, Henry," I said as I took the paper bag with my last name still stamped onto the side of it. "Be seeing you 'round."

"Tell your little mother hello for me."

"Will do." I waved as I walked away, and the bell jingled as I pulled the glass door toward me—a familiar sound, sometimes comforting, sometimes aggravating. Now I realized it was something I'd probably taken for granted. Like so many other things in my life. But today that little brass bell had the sound of finality to it. As if it was the end of an era. And maybe it was . . . *times they were a-changing*. Not that I wouldn't go back there to buy shoes again someday. I probably would. But this was the first time I'd ever been in Frederick's Fine Footwear when it hadn't belonged to my family. I think the whole thing just made me sad. Or maybe it was just something in the air that day.

I felt another wave of melancholy as I walked down the business loop, past other familiar shops, restaurants, my favorite bookstore . . . and although I'd walked this street hundreds of times before, I felt sort of like a stranger today. My family no longer owned the shoe store on the corner, my mother was selling the family home, and most of my old friends had moved on to jobs or had headed back to college to finish their degrees. Where did I fit in here now? Where did I fit in anywhere?

I gazed in the window at Harper's Cafe, trying to decide whether or not I was hungry since it was getting close to noon. But the window was grimy looking and uninviting, and their window display—a cluttered menagerie of crepe paper turkeys and cardboard pilgrims—wasn't particularly appetizing, although it did remind me that Thanksgiving was less than a week away. Mom had said that she wanted us to go down to Aunt Sally's in San Diego, which was fine with me since I had no other place to go anyway. Plus I hadn't seen my cousins in ages.

I continued walking until I reached Scott's Television and Appliance Shop, and that's when I observed several people clustered close to the large plate glass window out front. I wondered if Scott's had gotten in something new and amazing—maybe a color TV with stereo. But the small crowd was simply staring at an ordinary black-and-white television that was playing inside, and as usual, the sound was being piped through an outdoor speaker to the sidewalk. But I noticed the elderly woman had her hand clasped over her mouth and her eyes were wide with terror.

"Oh, no!" Mr. Garvey cried, the owner of the five-and-dime. *"No!"*

"It can't be," a woman next to him gasped.

"What?" I asked, but the small crowd was rushing into the shop.

"The president!" the elderly woman called over her shoulder.

"He's been shot!" Mr. Garvey said.

I followed them inside, where we all stood in silent horror, watching the nightmare unfolding before our very eyes. President John F. Kennedy had been shot while driving in a motorcade in Dallas, Texas. Everyone in the store was crying, including me. No one even tried to hide it. And I didn't care that I knew many of the people in the shop. I didn't care that I was supposed to be a grown man, a man who barely cried at his own father's funeral. I just stood there and openly sobbed with the rest of them. How could this have happened? In our own country? Our leader had been murdered, with his pretty young wife by his side. It was like a really bad movie.

I eventually left Scott's and spent the remainder of the day in a deep, dark depression. Tucked away in the gloomy warehouse, with my transistor radio blaring on an AM news station, I sat on a crate and listened to all the ongoing details of the assassination, the head wound, how long before

JFK died, how Vice President Johnson was sworn in on Air Force One before leaving Dallas—I took in the whole works. And finally, when I couldn't take it anymore, I started to play my piano. I played and played. And, although I knew it was senseless and would probably matter to no one but me, I dedicated my playing to President John Fitzgerald Kennedy and his two children and beautiful wife Jackie. My heart ached for all of them. How could something like this have happened?

It was about four o'clock when I finally remembered my own mother. I suddenly wondered how she would be taking all this—and realized that it might have hit her as hard as it hit me—and so I rushed home to find her sitting in front of the television with her hands in her lap and her big brown eyes all swollen and red from crying.

"Have you heard?" she whispered, clutching a white handkerchief in her fist and looking at me with a trembling chin.

Without saying anything, I nodded and sat down beside her. I draped one arm around her frail shoulders, and together we watched the news until finally she got up, went into the kitchen, and made us some supper. But neither of us felt hungry that night. We continued to watch the news on television, seeing that scene in the car again and again. Then we watched as they replayed the scene where Jackie stood by LBJ on Air Force One, watched as a new president was sworn in. We listened to the familiar newsmen, the ones who came on every evening at 6:00, but tonight they were discussing the terrifying events of the day and speculating over what would happen next, but it was impossible not to notice the sound of uncertainty, the uneasy caution in their voices, as if they too, like us, were afraid.

It wasn't until the next morning, Saturday, that I remembered to ask Mom about the sale of the house and whether or not the third time really had been the charm. She had already turned on the small television that Dad had insisted on putting in the kitchen, and I'm sure it was the first time I'd ever seen that television on, but the volume was turned down low.

"Yesterday?" she said as if it had been a few weeks ago. "Let's see . . . as I recall Jane had just told me that the couple liked the house and wanted to make an offer." She handed me a cup of coffee, setting the cow-shaped porcelain creamer on the table. "But that's when Sally called and told me about the shooting. She was crying and she said to turn on the television."

"And you did?"

She sighed. "Yes. Then we all just stood there in the family room and watched it. It was the strangest thing, Jamie. I'd only just met this couple and suddenly we were all sobbing and holding on to each other, like it was the end of the world and we were all we had. And then just as abruptly, they left, they wanted to go and get their children. I doubt they will want the house. Who can think of buying a house right now?"

I nodded. "It sure makes you look at life differently."

"I still can't believe it happened, Jamie."

"I know."

"He's really dead."

"I really liked Kennedy . . . I think he was the best president ever. No one can ever replace him."

"I know."

"I wanted to vote for him in the next election."

"It's all so sad." She stared down at her coffee cup.

"It was so cool having such a young president. It's like he understood young people. He wanted to make this country better."

"He was too young to die."

I swallowed hard. "Man, it just really ticks me off. And I know you don't want to hear this, Mom, but it really makes me want to join the Air Force more than ever now. I'm ready to give back to my country. I want to do it for JFK."

She nodded slightly, then looked away. I sensed she wasn't too pleased with my newfound resolve, but I could tell she didn't plan to stand against me either. At least not today.

The next few days felt like the entire country was draped in this ominous blanket of heavy darkness. Everyone seemed to be in mourning, or if they weren't, they at least had the good sense to keep their thoughts to themselves. The house was quiet and both Mom and I moved silently through the days. I was extra careful not to leave any dirty dishes on the counter, and I kept my personal items picked up, even put my dirty clothes in the laundry hamper in my room. I wasn't sure if I was growing up or if life had just suddenly gotten serious.

Finally, it was Thursday and Thanksgiving Day. Mom and I drove to San Diego, and we all did our best to "celebrate" the holiday, but even my cousins were much quieter than usual, a cloud of sadness hovered over everyone. I think we were all relieved when the day finally ended and we could put our party faces aside.

"Will we see you before the big trip?" Uncle Richard asked as we stood around my mom's white Caddie. He paused to light up a Marlborough, then took in a long drag.

"I don't know . . ." Mom jingled her keys in one hand.

"You don't still want to go over there now, do you?" Aunt Sally asked. "I thought maybe you'd changed your mind, Colleen . . . I mean with all that's happened and everything. Are you sure it's a good idea to travel now?"

"I don't know why not," Mom said. "What do you think, Richard? Any warnings about international travel?"

He shook his head, then let out a puff of smoke over his shoulder. "Not that I've heard. But make sure you check with your travel agent a day or two before you leave."

"Kennedy was Irish," I said suddenly. Of course, I instantly felt stupid for making such a childish-sounding statement, except that it had just occurred to me.

"That's right," Uncle Richard said, crushing the cigarette butt beneath the heel of his boot. "He was Irish-Catholic. First time ever in this country."

Then we all hugged and everyone said good-bye.

"They're okay," I said to Mom as she drove back up the freeway toward home.

"Yes, they are."

I decided it was some comfort to have family around at times like this. Especially since my dad was gone and he didn't really have much family still living, at least not around here. I know he had some relatives out on the East Coast, but they're like strangers to me. And the rest of my mom's family, except Aunt Sally, still live in Minnesota. I'd been out there once, back when I was about nine, before my

Grandpa Johnson died, and although there were lots and lots of cousins to play with, along with tons of other relatives, I pretty much felt like an outsider. Maybe it was because most of them had Johnson for a last name, the same name as the big family farm, and I didn't really fit in too well there.

So on Thanksgiving Day, less than a week after Kennedy was shot, I was glad to have Aunt Sally and Uncle Richard and my cousins around. And I was glad to have my mom too. Maybe that was one of the good things about a tragedy . . . it made you appreciate what you had.

5

Colleen

I made my best effort not to feel sorry for myself as Jamie and I walked through Los Angeles International Airport in mid-December. The terminal was busier than ever with all the holiday travelers, and everywhere I looked seemed to be wrapped in the trappings and trimmings of Christmas. From the oversized Christmas tree near the entrance, dripping in silver tinsel and blue lights, to Bing Crosby crooning "White Christmas" over the sound system, it was obvious that Christmas was just around the corner. They even had a Santa Claus wearing a flight jacket who was giving out candy canes and airline wings to young travelers.

And I think I could've dealt with all of that, if it hadn't been for all the families coming and going and saying goodbye to or greeting their loved ones. That was what got to me. Whether it was college students coming home for Christmas break or grandparents arriving with arms laden with brightly wrapped gifts—all the jubilant greetings and embraces and heading off for a joyous family reunion somewhere, well, it just got to me. And, as much as I despised self-pity or feeling like Ebenezer Scrooge, all that sweet Christmas cheer was hard to swallow.

Needless to say, I was greatly relieved when we were finally loaded onto our big jet, cozily buckled into our comfy seats, and being treated so nicely it was almost like being family. After we took off, I even allowed myself to imagine that the pretty blonde stewardess named Cindy was a relative, a cousin perhaps. And when she smiled and offered me hot tea, I actually pretended we were sitting in a parlor with a fire burning and a small pine Christmas tree in the corner.

"Do you need a blanket?" she asked Jamie with a sparkling Colgate smile. I could tell by the way she looked at him that she thought he was a nice-looking young man, and I had to agree with her on that account. And although she was probably at least ten years older than he, I could tell he was enjoying the attention.

"Sure," he said, taking the neatly folded plaid woolen throw from her. "Thank you."

"I think Cindy likes you," I whispered to Jamie as the stewardess walked away.

He looked slightly embarrassed, then grinned. "Maybe I should ask her out."

I made a slight face—a motherly expression meant as a subtle warning—then asked him what had become of his last girlfriend. "Wasn't her name Shelly?"

"Shelly," he said stiffly. "And that was almost two years ago, Mom."

I sensed a slight irritation in his voice, as if Shelly was an unpleasant subject, but since I also knew we'd be stuck together for some time and conversation topics might possibly get scarce, I decided why not persist a bit. Besides, I was curious about the girlfriend. He had even talked about bringing her home to visit at one time and then that was it—not another word on the subject. Of course, Hal had passed away about the same time and life got a little stressful after that. Perhaps I'd missed something. And that made me feel sad . . . like a poor excuse for a mother. But now I really wanted to know. Not that I could force my son to talk. But I could try. Just as I was formulating my next question, Cindy returned.

"We have complimentary champagne," she said, flashing that brilliant smile again. I started to decline on her offer, but then remembered that this was going to be a long flight and perhaps a little champagne would make things more comfortable for both Jamie and me—might even loosen our tongues a bit.

"That sounds lovely," I said. "How about you, Jamie?"

He grinned and nodded eagerly. Although my son had been twenty-one for months now, it still felt strange to think that he was of legal drinking age and could casually drink a glass of champagne with me right now. Hadn't he just been learning to ride a two-wheeler last week? And when did he get his braces off? Suddenly everything about motherhood and raising my only son felt like a fast hazy blur—similar to the clouds that were passing by the window at the moment.

"Here you go," Cindy said, handing us both a glass of champagne.

We thanked her, and then I held up my glass to Jamie. "Here's to a good trip."

"To Ireland."

We clinked glasses, and despite my lapse in matters of faith these past couple of years and particularly recently, I actually said a silent little prayer just then. *God, if you're there, if you can hear me and you're not too busy, please, help this trip to turn out right. So much is at stake . . . please, please, help me. Amen.*

"So . . . ," I said to Jamie, as we were finishing our champagne, "I'm curious as to what became of Shelly."

He downed the remainder of his drink. "She went her way . . . I went mine."

"So, it was a congenial parting?"

He shrugged in a way that suggested it was not. Then Cindy reappeared with her bottle of champagne. "More?"

Jamie stuck his glass out, and thinking it couldn't hurt our conversation, I followed his lead. Then when we were about halfway through our second glass, I tried again, deciding that if he really didn't want to talk about Shelly, I would simply change the subject. But to my amazement, he began to open up.

"It was really her idea to break up," he said quietly.

I just nodded, trying to look empathetic but not overly so.

"It was right after Christmas break, back in '61. I was so glad to get back to school and see her again. I'd been wishing that I'd invited her to come home with me during the holidays, to meet you and Dad . . ." He kind of sighed now. "Turned out I was a day late and a dollar short."

"Why's that?"

"During Christmas break, Shelly had gotten back together with an old high school sweetheart who'd been going to an Ivy League school back east."

"Oh . . ."

"Yeah, she told me that this guy had always been the love of her life and that he'd broken up with her to go to college, but then when they got together again, he suddenly decided she was really the one for him and they'd actually gotten engaged on Christmas Eve." He shook his head. "Can you believe that?"

"Seems like pretty fast work, not to mention a little harsh," I said defensively. "Especially since she'd been dating you."

"Yeah, you'd think she might've called me or something."

"Well, I don't mean to sound callous, Jamie, but I'm not too sure I'd like this girl. She sounds a little fickle to me. I think you deserve someone better."

"Yeah, but you never met her, Mom." His voice got that defensive edge to it again, just like when he was in high school and I questioned him on something. "She was actually very nice—smart and pretty. Everyone who knew her liked her a lot. Some of the guys in my dorm were pretty jealous of me for going with her." He paused and got a thoughtful look. "I think I might've asked her to marry me."

Well, I knew I'd stuck my foot in my mouth now. But, at the same time, I was glad that he was being so open with me. Whether it was the champagne or being away from home, it didn't matter, we were actually talking and not arguing! And yet, at the same time, my heart ached for my son. I wanted to hug him and tell him everything would be okay; I wanted to put a bandage on his owie and kiss it and make it all better. Wasn't that what mothers did when their sons were hurting? But I realized things had changed. Jamie wasn't my little boy anymore.

"She sounds like a nice girl," I finally said, "and, of course, I can't imagine you caring for a girl who wasn't nice. I'm sure that I probably would've liked her too. But I do feel badly that she hurt you like that, Jamie. I can't help feeling like a mom, you know. It's just the way God wires us."

He nodded now. "It was hard losing her, Mom."

"I'm sure it was . . ."

Then he turned and looked at me with those clear blue eyes, so striking against his dark brown hair, so reminiscent that it was painful to look at sometimes. "Did anything like that ever happen to you? Any broken hearts in your past?"

I took a quick sip of champagne, gauging my time and asking myself if this was the right moment or not. I just wasn't sure. Or maybe I just wasn't ready.

"I mean, I know that Dad was head over heels in love with you," he said quickly, relieving me of having to give an answer. "I could see it in the way he treated you, Mom. I don't know if you always saw it, but I'd see him looking at you, and it was as if he had stars in his eyes. The guy adored you, Mom. And I remember, not that long before he died, Dad was talking about how you guys met when you came to apply for a job at the shoe store, and how it was love at first sight for him, and how even though you didn't know the first thing about shoes, he hired you right on the spot. And he even confessed at how stunned he'd been when you actually agreed to marry him. I think he said he was 'over the moon for you.'" Jamie laughed. "That was pretty good for Dad, don't you think?"

I nodded, moved by my son's sentiment and blinking back hot tears that brimmed in my eyes. But, although touched, I also felt as if someone had just twisted a dull knife in my heart. I knew that Jamie would assume my tears were for Hal, because I missed him. And that was partially true. I was extremely sad that Hal was gone, and I did miss him. Every single day. There was no denying that. But in that moment, I felt like a complete hypocrite, and my heart ached with an old festering guilt—a guilt I could never seem to completely shake off. And that was because I still faulted myself with the fact that I had never been "over the moon" for Hal.

Oh, I had tried my hardest, I'd put on a good show, I'd been the best wife I knew how to be, and yet, in my mind, it was never enough. Never equal to what Hal poured out over me. His love for me was so natural, so easy. Sometimes it reminded me of a dance. He knew all the steps, he moved gracefully, effortlessly . . . and I sort of stumbled along. I never felt equal to him when it came to loving. And with him gone now, I felt even more like a failure—a phony. And I feared this shroud of guilt would follow me to my grave and perhaps even haunt me thereafter.

"Dad was a good guy, Mom," Jamie continued as if to comfort me, still misunderstanding my emotions. "I mean, I probably took him for granted more than anyone, and I really do regret that. But I've been thinking about him a lot lately . . . especially since President Kennedy was killed. I've been thinking about a lot of stuff. Like what it takes to become a really good man, you know, someone like Dad or JFK. And I think about what a good example Dad gave me—he was honest and hardworking and really kind. He was a great husband to you. I couldn't have asked for a better dad. Man, I still remember how he'd close up the shoe store early just so he could come see me at a ball game."

"He loved watching you play sports, Jamie. He'd never been very good at them himself. You brought a lot of joy into his life."

"And I want to make him proud, I really do."

"I know you do."

"And I think he'd be proud if I joined the Air Force. Like maybe I'd be fulfilling his dream somehow. You know?"

I swallowed hard, then nodded. This was a battlefield I wasn't ready for.

"Anyway, I realize how lucky I was to have him. We were both lucky."

"Or as your dad would say, we were blessed."

"Yeah, *blessed*."

A hot tear escaped, sliding down my cheek now. Using the cocktail napkin, I dabbed at it. "You're right, your dad was a good man. And he loved us both dearly."

"And, even though I acted like a jerk sometimes and I know I hurt him about the shoe business and everything, I really did love him." His eyes got a little moist too. "Do you think he really knew that?"

I nodded. *"He knew."* I closed my eyes and leaned my head back, trying to contain the tears that threatened to flood. Jamie's words felt like iodine being poured into a deep wound—they burned like fire, but hopefully there was healing in them too. Still, this wasn't going to make it any easier to tell him the truth—the timing seemed all wrong just now. Maybe once we were in Ireland it would be easier. *God, give me strength!*

6

Jamie

I thought flying was fun when we started out on this trip. But by the time we landed in Dublin, I didn't think I'd be wanting to get on a plane anytime soon. "I'm glad that's over with," I told Mom as we gathered our bags. "I'm sick of planes."

"I am too," she said. "I never breathed so much cigarette smoke in my life, not even on our trip to Paris, which I'd thought was bad enough. But I think most of the passengers must've been smokers on this flight."

"Well, at least we don't have to fly again for a couple of weeks."

"Actually, that's not the plan," she said as we waited for a cab. We were trying to stay close to the building to avoid the rain that seemed to be coming down in buckets just now. "We do have another short flight on Tuesday."

"Where to?"

"Galway."

"What's in Galway?"

She shrugged and waved to an oncoming cab. "I guess we'll find out."

Then suddenly we were loading our bags in the trunk and jumping into the back of the cab. We were both dripping wet as the cabby drove us into the city, and Mom was getting more and more frustrated as she tried to make herself clear to the driver, who appeared to be a bit deaf. Mom was using far too many words and actually trying to give the cabby directions, which seemed a bit crazy, plus I could tell the poor guy was ready to toss us out, fare or no fare. It didn't help matters that his thick accent was impossible for Mom to decipher, although the more they bantered, the more I seemed to be getting it. That was when I realized that Mom's ear was not too clever when it came to accents and decided to jump in.

"Why don't you let me translate for you?" I teased.

She scowled at me, but handed me the paper with the name of the hotel and other details written on it.

"The Fitzwilliam Hotel," I said as clearly as possible, even trying to sound a bit Irish myself.

He nodded. "Aye, 'at's on Sain' Stephens Green, i'tiz."

"Yes," I said eagerly. "I mean *aye*! That's it!"

Then he laughed and drove on through the dark and damp city, and soon we were pulling up to a well-lit hotel. At that point, I decided to take charge of matters. I'd already exchanged a couple of twenties at the airport, and after a quick inventory of the strange-looking Irish bills and coins, I managed to pay and tip the cabby. It was possible I over-tipped him, because he seemed pretty happy, but at least we were safely at the hotel and the guy was very helpful in getting our bags into the lobby.

Mom smiled at me as she removed and shook out her trench coat. "I'll have to remember to take you on all my foreign travels."

"You planning on doing a lot of this?" I asked as I removed my soggy suede jacket and laid it over a suitcase.

"You never know." Then she glanced up to the registration desk. "Would you like to help check us in too?"

"Sure."

Then she handed me a confirmation slip. "Tell them we have a reservation for three nights, adjoining rooms."

Mom listened as I spoke to the man at the desk. This guy was a little easier to understand, and I suspect that she could've handled it just fine. But it was sort of fun taking charge, and I could tell she was getting a kick out of it too.

"I know I should be exhausted," I told Mom as we rode up the elevator, which they call a *lift*, "but I think I've gotten my second wind. I wouldn't mind taking a little stroll and checking out the nightlife."

She frowned. "In the rain?"

"Sure. Isn't that what Ireland is all about?"

She sort of laughed. "Well, count me out. All I want is a hot bath and a soft bed and maybe a little room service."

"See you in the morning then?" I said, after I got her bags and things into her room, which actually looked pretty nice. Mom was doing this thing first class.

"You be careful out there, Jamie," she warned as she hung up her trench coat. "I know you're twenty-one and think you're all grown up, but you're also a stranger in a foreign country and—"

"I know"—I held up my hand—"don't be taking any wooden nickels."

She sort of smiled. "Just be careful."

I gave her a slight salute. "Will do."

I dumped my stuff on the floor of my room, which was also pretty ritzy, then dug a dry shirt out of my big suitcase and found a slightly wrinkled sports jacket, and then I took off. I didn't know much about Dublin, but something about the look of the city as the cabby drove us here pulled me right in. I couldn't wait to do a little exploring.

I walked around for about half an hour, just enjoying the opportunity to stretch my legs and get the lead out. I passed by numerous pubs and considered going into several, but it wasn't until I heard lively music coming out of Flannery's that I decided to go in. Now, I'd never heard Irish music before, not that I could recall anyway, but something about the sound of this band felt familiar. And something about the music just drew me in. I bought myself a pint of Guinness, took a seat near the band, and just listened.

It wasn't long before I was conversing with the three guys in the band, just talking about regular stuff between songs—music talk. They thought it was cool that I was an American and a musician, and I thought it was cool that they were Irish. Sure, that made no sense to them since they were, obviously, in Ireland. But it was as if I was getting pulled into this country—and its music. Something about the whole place just seemed right to me. After about an hour, I offered to buy the guys in the band a Guinness, and they gladly agreed. It seems musicians didn't get rich in this country either.

Sean, the outgoing redhead, played the fiddle. Galen, the short, quiet guy, played the drum. In fact he played several drums, but only one at a time. And Galen's drums were nothing like the trap set that Steve had used for Jamie and the Muskrats. These Irish drums resembled oversized tambourines, but without the jingles on the sides. And Galen played them with a collection of sticks, resulting in a variety of cool sounds. Last but not least was Mick, the leader. He played both the guitar and a flutelike instrument that he called a *penny whistle*.

We talked about music while drinking our Guinness, and to my surprise, we were all pretty interested in a new British group, The Beatles. Mick had even heard them play once in Germany.

"'Twas afore they got their new drummer," he told me with a thick Irish accent.

"Wha' is the name of the drummer?" Galen asked. "'Twas a strange un, I recall."

"Ringo?" Mick offered.

"That's right," Galen said. "Ringo! Now, where'd they come up with that?"

We were so engrossed in our conversation that the pub owner had to remind them it was time to play again. So I sat and listened some more. And they finally wrapped it up a little before midnight. By then I was actually starting to get a little sleepy, probably jet-lagged, or maybe it was that third pint of Guinness. But since the guys offered me a ride, I didn't mind waiting for them to pack it up. I couldn't help but wonder what Mom would think of my new group of friends—not that she'd still be up to see them—but I felt sure she'd think they were a little strange with their long hair and sideburns. But then Mom wasn't used to musicians either.

As we rode in their van back to my hotel, Sean and I got to talking about the recent assassination of President Kennedy. It seemed the Irish had been almost as upset by this as the Americans. Then Sean told me about his hometown.

"I grew up in ta very same place where John Fitzgerald Kennedy's ancestors come from," he said proudly.

"Really?" I was impressed. "What's it called?"

"New Ross in Wexford."

"Where's that?" I asked, wishing I'd brought my map of Ireland along.

"Near a city called Waterford," Sean said as he lit a cigarette. "Not far from Dublin. Ya take the train, an' 'tis only a day trip."

"There ya go now," Galen called from the driver's seat, which was oddly on the right side of the cab. "The Fitzwilliam 'otel."

Sean whistled. "Quite posh. You must be rich."

I laughed and confessed I was traveling with my mom. That made them laugh. But they all slapped me on the back and told me to come back to Flannery's and see them again.

"We're featured for a fortnight," Galen said as I hopped out.

"Big New Year's Eve bash," Sean called out.

"I'll be back," I promised. "Count on it!"

Then I ran through the rain up to the hotel, rode up the lift, and let myself into my room. I considered checking on

Mom, but figured she'd be dead asleep by now. Hopefully she hadn't stayed up and worried about me, but just in case she was still awake and listening, I tried not to be too quiet in my room. That should set her mind at ease.

By the time I hit the sack, I was so exhausted that my eyes couldn't even stay open. It'd been an unexpectedly groovy evening, my first night in Ireland, and already I'd met some fun musicians. But what surprised me most was how much I liked Ireland, when I hadn't even wanted to come here in the first place. I don't think I could begin to explain what was going on in me, not even to myself—but something about this country felt comfortable, familiar even. It was weird but cool.

I replayed some of our conversations from tonight, thinking that if I really worked on it, I might be able to get down that Irish accent a little before we headed back home. In a way there was something almost musical about their language, and something about the sound of it—or perhaps it was the rhythm, it was hard to understand . . . but it made my fingers just itch to get to a piano. Maybe it was a combination of the music I'd heard tonight, the guys I'd talked to, and the country itself, but somehow I knew this experience was changing me as a musician, and it might even change the way I played piano. In fact, I was so jazzed that, although I was totally beat, I didn't know if I could even go to sleep.

7

Colleen

It took me a few minutes to get my bearings and remember where I was, but then it hit me—*Ireland*! I was really here. I glanced at the little alarm clock to see it was past ten and felt surprised that I slept so long. Then I remembered how I woke in the middle of the night, how I worried that Jamie might not have made it back to the hotel safely. But I'd been unwilling to knock on his door and disturb him in case I was wrong, so I just sat and watched the hands slowly moving around the clock, and then I paced back and forth in the room and asking myself, why had I come here? I finally forced myself back to bed again. But I still felt anxious and uneasy, fretting that it had been a big mistake to take this expensive trip, fearing that nothing was going to help me tell Jamie the news that I felt certain he would never want to hear.

But with morning here and the Irish sun shining through the heavy lace curtains, I began to feel better. Perhaps it wasn't a mistake after all. Funny how the nighttime turns challenges into monsters. I did a few stretches and tried to calculate what time it was in Pasadena right now, but then decided, why bother? This was Ireland and I was on Irish time, might as well get used to it.

As I slipped on my quilted satin robe, I noticed a white piece of paper by my door, as if someone had slipped it under from the hallway. I went over to pick it up, seeing the word "Mom" penned across the front. Obviously it was from Jamie. I hoped nothing was wrong.

> Dear Mom,
> I had a fantastic time last night. I met some musicians and they told me about the town where John F. Kennedy's family came from. I got up early so that I could look into taking the train there. I think I'll be back sometime tonight. I hope you don't mind.
> Love, Jamie

I reread the note and wondered what kind of wild-goose chase my son had taken off on today, and who on earth were these "musicians" and how had he met them so quickly? Young people these days—it almost made my head spin. But then I reminded myself that Jamie was an adult, and if he was old enough to join the Air Force, which I hoped I'd be able to dissuade him from doing, then he was certainly old enough to hop on an Irish train and see the sites. Besides, I told myself, as I leisurely bathed and dressed, a quiet day to myself wouldn't be so bad. Perhaps I would explore a bit of Dublin. Maybe even do some shopping. I'd promised Sally to look for some fisherman knit sweaters, and I'd heard there was beautiful crystal to be found in this country. Then, by evening, Jamie would return and we could have a nice dinner somewhere. I'd ask the concierge downstairs to recommend a good place.

After a light breakfast of a soft-boiled egg, served in a fragile porcelain eggcup, which was a new experience for me, along with toast and delicious jam and some nice Irish tea, I decided it was time to see a bit of Dublin. Dressed warmly and armed with my umbrella and trench coat, since it had just started to rain again, I inquired at the concierge desk. Fortunately, this man's accent was easier for me to understand. Plus, I knew it was good practice.

"I've heard Dublin has some good museums."

"Aye, we do. All sorts of museums. History and art. What sort of things are you interested in?"

"I like art," I said. "Not that I'm much of an expert. But I did enjoy seeing the Louvre in Paris." I remembered how Hal had patiently accompanied me that day. The poor man really didn't care much for art, although he appreciated the architecture.

"Do you like modern art?" he asked hopefully. "We have a wonderful place."

I wasn't terribly fond of modern styles like cubism or Picasso, but his enthusiasm caught me off guard. "Sure," I said.

Then he told me the name, which was quite a mouthful. "But you'll need a cab," he said as he pulled out a city map and pointed out some other sites as well as the better shopping areas that I might be interested in. Then he had one of the bellboys call a cab for me, and I set out for what I hoped would be a delightful adventure.

Unfortunately, within minutes I began to wish I had Jamie along to help "translate." The cabby, like the one last night, had a heavy Irish accent, and it seemed the harder I tried to understand him, the worse it got. Finally, I pulled out a fountain pen and a piece of notepaper from the hotel and wrote down exactly where I wished to go, *The Hugh Lane Municipal Gallery of Modern Art*. The note did just the trick, and before long I was dropped off by an old but impressive-looking building. And to my delight, the "modern art" in this museum featured some of my all-time favorite artists, including Monet, Degas, and Manet. I suddenly began to appreciate Ireland's history, realizing that the interpretation for "modern" was all a matter of perspective. To Ireland, an old country, these impressionist painters were considered "modern."

After that, I took another cab over to the National Museum of Ireland. The art museum had whet my appetite, and I was now intrigued by Ireland and its history. The museum was quiet, and other than a surprisingly well-behaved class of elementary school children, I had the place almost entirely to myself. So I took my time as I studied ancient weapons, beautifully carved furniture, silver and gold sculptures, ceramics and glassware, as well as lots of other things.

For some reason I felt particularly taken by the Irish harps, or perhaps it was their history. I learned that England, in an attempt to oppress Ireland, had banned the harp several hundred years earlier. The ruling Brits feared the Irish's love of harp music would lead to nationalism, and so they killed all the harpists and burned their harps. It broke my heart to think of that sweet music being stolen from the Irish like that—it felt so wrong, criminal even. However, I discovered that the Irish did salvage some of their lost music by gathering the few surviving harpists and secretly having them write down what music they could remember. I supposed it had been better than nothing, but so much of the music, not to mention those ancient harps, had been completely lost. Such a shame.

With a sense of melancholy, I decided to take advantage of the break in weather by walking back to my hotel. It was nearly one now, and I was hoping that Jamie might've gotten back earlier than expected. But there was no sign of him. I asked the concierge about the place where our former president's family had immigrated from, and he told me that it was near the town of Waterford.

"Where they make crystal?" I said.

"Aye. And there are bus tours that go up there." He pulled out a brochure and handed it to me. "If you'd like to see the factory."

"I'll think about that," I told him. Then I returned to the hotel restaurant and ordered some lunch. It felt odd eating alone for the second time today. I didn't like to think of myself as a needy sort of woman, the kind who must always have a man in tow to feel at ease, but suddenly I wasn't so sure. Hal had always taken such good care of me. He was the kind of man who opened doors, took me by the arm, carried my bags, and just generally made my life smoother. It hadn't been easy getting used to taking care of myself this past year and a half. And yet, I felt I'd made progress. I felt that I was getting more comfortable with my widowed status. Still, would I have attempted this trip on my own? Having Jamie along had seemed to make it easier, but then he certainly was nowhere to be seen today. I hoped that all was well with him. And, again, I told myself that it was for the best. We both needed our space today. Perhaps it would bolster my spirits and help me to say the things that needed saying.

Following lunch, and a continued break in the wet weather, I walked over to a couple of sites that weren't too far from the hotel. I toured the National Museum until I felt as if I'd absorbed as much art and history as was possible. After that, I found my way to a nice little shopping district. The one thing I had learned in my world travels (although relatively few) was that shopping, particularly for women, came easy, it seemed we all spoke the same language when it came to opening up one's pocketbook and purchasing something. Shopkeepers were always friendly and willing to take time to explain things like merchandise quality, money exchange rates, or even fashion tips. And so by the end of my day, I had splurged on several fisherman knit sweaters, two mohair blankets, and other various Irish souvenirs. Most of these I had sent to Sally and her family, although it was doubtful that they would make it by Christmas. Still, it saved me from having to pack them about the country for two weeks. The rest of the items I'd had sent along to the hotel.

My biggest splurges of the day came from a shop that specialized in Donegal tweed. Ireland is known for its fine wool, and Donegal is considered the best. For Jamie, I purchased a brown tweed sports coat that I knew would look handsome on him. For myself, I was easily talked into a classy black-and-white hound's-tooth suit.

"Miss Doris Day, herself, purchased the exact same suit," she assured me.

"Really?" I said, not sure that I believed her, or that I really cared.

"'Tis lovelier on you," she said in a hushed tone, as if Doris herself was in the next dressing room. That was when I knew this saleslady was good. Still, I had to agree with her, the suit did look awfully nice on me.

"I'll take it," I told her.

"We have a lovely Irish linen blouse that is perfect with this suit."

Naturally, I was a pushover. But, all in all, it was a wonderful way to spend my first full day in Ireland. And it helped to distract me from worrying about Jamie. At least for the time being. However, when I got back to the hotel and it was after five and dark outside and, according to the front desk, Jamie still hadn't returned, I wasn't sure what to think. So I wrote out a message and handed it to the clerk.

"Please give this to my son when he gets in." I wasn't going to take any chances of missing Jamie. I could imagine my wayward boy getting in and then popping back out without even letting me know that he'd gotten safely back to town. Jamie had always been a fairly independent boy, but he'd gotten even more so once he'd gone off to college. Not that I minded—I thought independence and confidence were good traits. But sometimes I did worry about him. For instance, the weeks preceding this trip . . . even though Jamie had been helpful at home, he'd also been known to disappear without telling me he'd even gone, and sometimes for hours at a time. And if I'd ask him where he'd been, or what he'd been doing, or who he'd been with, Jamie would often turn evasive and defensive, as if it were none of my business.

It wasn't that I thought he'd been up to no good, but I was curious. And I was aware that many of his friends didn't live in town anymore, and I couldn't help but wonder what it was he did with his spare time. Goodness, wasn't that what mothers were supposed to do? Just because our children grew older didn't mean we quit worrying, did it?

I went up to my room and began to put away today's purchases. I paused to take out the lovely mohair blanket that I'd gotten for myself. I shook it out and admired its colors, a delightful mix of mossy greens and rusty reds, then laid it across a chair. It would be nice to have this throw on these long Irish winter nights. The climate was so different than Southern California. Then I removed my new tweed suit from the box and carefully hung it up in the closet. Very classy. And then, because it was chilly in the room, I slipped on the cardigan fisherman knit sweater and checked it in the mirror. I hadn't intended on getting one for myself and hadn't even tried it on at the shop, but after finding lovely ones for my sister and her family, and a pullover for Jamie, I thought, why not? And, as I studied my reflection, I thought perhaps I'd made the right choice after all. It really did look rather good on me. I think it actually made me look younger. I struck a pose, putting one hand on my hip and jutting my chin out like a model, then laughed at myself. Sally had always thought that I looked like Audrey Hepburn, although I felt sure she was only being nice. Still there was something about this sweater with my dark hair pinned up in a French roll that almost made me think there was a faint resemblance.

Finally, it was half past seven and I still hadn't heard a word from Jamie. I'd tried knocking on his door, but no answer. I even called down to the front desk; no one had seen him. Now I hated feeling like a fretful granny, but I couldn't help but begin to imagine the worst. After all, we were in a foreign country—who knew what could go wrong? What if something terrible had happened or what if he were unconscious and no one knew who to contact for him? It wasn't as if my son was wearing a dog tag, and even his California driver's license would be useless in reaching me here in Dublin. Why hadn't I thought of this before?

What if Jamie had been robbed at knifepoint? Or kidnapped by Irish thugs? Or hit by a car? I'd heard stories of American tourists who had stepped straight into oncoming traffic, all because they were looking the wrong way, left instead of right. Oh, why hadn't I thought to warn him about that sort of thing? Soon I was pacing again, fretting and pacing, pacing and fretting. And finally I knew that the only thing I could really do was to pray. I remembered how often Hal had told me this very thing. "Don't worry, Honey," he'd say calmly if Jamie had stayed out a little late when he was still a teen. "Pray instead." But Hal's faith had been stronger than mine. His experience with God had seemed more genuine than my own. And it was in moments like this that I dearly missed that man. And so I prayed. And before long I did begin to feel calmer.

At eight o'clock, I called for room service. Although I didn't feel hungry, I thought a light meal could be a distraction. I ordered the lentil soup and a Caesar salad and hot tea. I was sitting alone in my room, barely touching my food, when I heard a knock at the door. Preparing myself for the worst, perhaps a policeman to inform me of an accident, I went to answer it.

"Hi, Mom!" Jamie said cheerfully. His cheeks were ruddy and his dark hair was curling from the moisture in the air. Suddenly I was torn between wanting to take him over my knee, or to simply hug him. Fortunately hugging won out. Although it was a damp hug.

"Where have you been?" I demanded as I pulled him into the room. "I've been worried sick." I used the linen napkin from my neglected meal to wipe my eyes, trying to conceal the fact that tears of relief were falling.

"Sorry, Mom. Didn't you get my note?"

"Yes. But you said you'd be home this evening."

"It is *this evening*."

I nodded. "Yes, I suppose so. But I guess I thought you'd be home in time for dinner."

"I actually sort of thought I would too." He glanced over to my tray. "Sorry about that."

"It's okay. I'm just glad you're safely back. Do you want to order room service?"

Soon we both had a tray of food. I ordered something more tempting than my lukewarm lentil soup, and we sat in my room, eating happily together, and Jamie told me all about his excursion. And I told him about mine.

"I think we both had lovely days," I had to admit as I went to get the items I'd purchased for him.

"Yeah, it's pretty amazing, Mom," he said with a youthful enthusiasm—a tone I hadn't heard in his voice, it seemed, in years. "I really like this place—I feel like I fit in here—in Ireland, I mean. I can't even explain it really, but it's groovy."

I suppressed a smile as I handed him the pullover. "I like Ireland too, and this is a *real* Irish fisherman knit sweater."

"For me?" He stood to examine it better.

"When in Ireland . . ."

He quickly pulled the sweater over his head, emerging with a big grin and ruffled hair. "How's it look?"

"Perfect," I said. "Very handsome."

"But do I look Irish?" he asked hopefully.

I nodded, hoping I wouldn't start crying again. "Oh, yes, very much so."

"Cool."

Then I showed him the tweed jacket, which fit him perfectly and actually gave him the appearance of a young country gentleman. "They say that Donegal wool can last for decades," I told him. "If you take care of it properly. The tag tells how."

"Thanks, Mom. I really like it." But it was the sweater that he put back on. "I was thinking about going down to that pub again tonight. It's called Flannery's and it's about a thirty-minute walk from the hotel. That Irish band is going to be there all month, and I really wanted to hear them again. Do you want to come along?"

I considered this. On the one hand, I felt flattered that he was actually inviting me. On the other hand, it was past nine now, and it had already been a very long day. That, combined with my worrying this evening, and I felt exhausted. "Maybe not tonight," I said. "I'm still a little jet-lagged plus I didn't sleep too well last night."

He nodded. "Man, was I surprised that I slept like a baby. Then I got up feeling great. I think this Irish air agrees with me."

I smiled. "Well, it's probably a lot cleaner than Southern California. But it's a lot cooler too."

"This sweater will be just the thing for that. Thanks again!"

"I'm glad you like it, Jamie. And have a good time tonight, but do be careful, okay?" Then, even though I didn't want to sound like a complete worrywart, I warned him to remember that the traffic came from the opposite direction. "Tourists have been known to get killed after looking the wrong way and then stepping out."

He just laughed. "Yeah, I know, Mom. I already figured it out."

Then, just like that, he was gone and I was alone again. And although I was hugely relieved that he'd made it back safely, and that he'd had a great day, I also felt like I might've missed an opportunity just now. I considered his high interest in Ireland, how much he seemed to love everything about the country and, well, it seemed like it had been my perfect chance to tell him the truth—to just get it over with. Then, I reminded myself, we still have lots of time, nearly two weeks. Maybe the smart thing would be to simply let Jamie have a good time, to experience the culture, the people, and to completely fall in love with the country. And then, when the timing was perfect and he was ready to hear the truth, then I would tell him.

8

Jamie

On our second day in Ireland, Mom showed me the sites in Dublin, which was actually somewhat interesting. Then on our third day, we rode the train to Waterford to see the crystal factory. To my surprise that was fairly interesting too. Then on Tuesday, after I had a late night listening to the guys at Flannery's again, we got up early and flew in a small plane to Galway, then got onto a bus that was headed to a region called Connemara. Mom seemed to have it all worked out, and I couldn't help but be curious.

"So, what's in Connemara anyway?" I asked her as I looked out the fogged-up window to see lots of green rolling hills and soggy-looking sheep.

She shrugged in a slightly mysterious way. "To tell you the truth, I don't really know," she admitted. "I just heard about it once and wanted to see it for myself. Some people call Connemara the Emerald of the Isle, and I've heard it's supposed to be incredibly beautiful." Then she told me how an old John Wayne movie had been filmed somewhere around there. "I just loved that movie."

"A *Western*?" I stared in disbelief. Mom usually went out of her way to avoid watching any kind of Western, and it was Dad who'd been the John Wayne fan.

"Of course not. A Western in Ireland? No, John Wayne played a prizefighter from America who came over here and fell in love with an Irish lass. It was a charming movie."

"Oh."

"I can hardly believe it's only a week before Christmas," Mom said.

"Yeah, they don't seem to make nearly as big of a deal of it as they do in America. I almost forgot it was the holidays."

"I have noticed an occasional wreath here or there, or a small Christmas tree in a shop," she pointed out.

"But not all the trappings and trimmings that get plastered all over the place back home. And none of that tinny old music."

"I think it's rather refreshing. I get so tired of all the commercialism and the pressure to do so much in so little time. By the time you decorate and send out cards and make cookies and buy far too many gifts and go to parties and cook a big dinner, it's practically over with and you're completely worn out. I don't recall it being anything like that when I was growing up. In fact, my parents always kept the holidays fairly simple, a candlelight service on Christmas Eve and a nice family dinner on Christmas. Besides a tree and a few gifts, it wasn't such a big ordeal back then."

"So, what are we doing for Christmas?"

Mom frowned slightly. "To be honest, I don't really know, Jamie. I guess I hadn't really thought that out. Of course, we'll be at the hotel in Clifden all week. But maybe we can find a church with a Christmas Eve service." She got a wistful look. "Perhaps a candlelight service like when I was a girl."

"Yeah, I guess that could be interesting."

"And then we'll find a nice restaurant for Christmas Day. I wonder what the Irish eat for Christmas . . . maybe the fatted goose and plum pudding, or is that British?"

"What if all the restaurants are closed?"

Mom's brow creased now. "Oh, dear, I hadn't even considered that."

Now I felt bad for worrying her. "We'll figure it out," I said quickly. "Worst-case scenario, we'll get provisions from a grocery store and just make do. Have an indoor picnic or something in our hotel room."

She smiled now. "That sounds like fun."

Mom returned to writing postcards and I continued to watch out the window. It really was beautiful landscape, so green that it seemed almost unreal. At first the clouds had hung so low that they gave the countryside a misty, almost haunted appearance, but after a while they began to lift and eventually the rain shower quit as well. I'd already heard that this was one of the wettest spots in the world, and I'd started to wonder if we'd ever see blue sky again, but by the time we reached our destination, the small seaport town of Clifden, the sun had actually made an appearance.

The bus dropped us right in front of our hotel, which was on the main drag, and the driver even helped us get our bags inside. On the way into town, I'd noticed there were several pubs, and one of them had a sign that said LIVE MUSIC, and I was eager to check that out.

"This looks like a cool little town," I said to Mom after we got checked in and were riding an ancient elevator up to our floor. I hoped the tiny "lift," loaded with us and our bags, wasn't going to give out before we reached the third floor.

"I think I'll be taking the stairs after that ride," I told Mom when we finally got out.

"It'd probably be quicker," she said as she handed me a large brass key. "You're in 302 and I'm in 304. And there are no phones in the rooms."

"How about TVs?" I joked. Even our big hotel in Dublin didn't have televisions in the rooms.

"I think I'll put my stuff away, then check out the town," I told Mom as I unlocked my door. "How about you?"

"I might take a little walk," she said. "Maybe mail my postcards. And I'd like to find a bookshop since I finished my paperback."

"Want to meet up for dinner?"

"Yes, that sounds good. How about 6:30 in the lobby downstairs? Maybe one of us will find a promising restaurant by then."

I tossed my bags into the room, then closed and locked the door. "See ya," I called as I headed for the stairway. I wanted to check out that pub, the one with the live music sign. Hopefully I could talk Mom into going there tonight. But, even more than that, I wanted to find someplace with a piano. Maybe there was a music store in town. Or maybe one of the pubs would have a piano. Perhaps I could offer to play for a Guinness. I laughed to myself as I hurried down the street. Or maybe they would offer me a Guinness to quit playing.

The wet sidewalks were steaming in the afternoon sun, and the temperature felt warmer than it had in days. But it was the air that got my attention. It smelled so fresh and good, breezing in right off the sea, I thought that if a person could bottle this and sell it, they would soon become rich.

I ducked into the first pub and looked around to see if there was a piano in sight, but no luck. I checked several others, but again no luck. Even the one with the live music sign was pianoless.

"Whad'ya 'ave?" the man behind the bar asked.

"A piano?"

He laughed. "Is that some fancy American drink?"

I shook my head, then pantomimed playing a piano. "No, I was just looking for a piano that I could practice on. Is there a music store in town?"

He scratched his head. "Aye, but I don't tink O'Toole's got any pianos in his wee store."

"How about the pubs?" I persisted. "Do any have pianos?"

Now his eyes lit up. "Up at the Anchor Inn is a nice grand piano."

"Where's that?"

"Ya take the beach road an'ya go on up past the yacht club and a bit beyond there and you'll see a tall brick building with lots of windows, that be the Anchor Inn. The menu's a bit pricey, but the food's good and there's a nice view up there, if ya go afore dark, that is."

I thanked him and started walking toward the sea, figuring that must be the right direction for the beach road. It took about an hour to find the place, but sure enough there was a nice grand piano sitting in the corner of the restaurant. Other than a couple of old guys sitting at the bar on the other side of the room, the place looked pretty deserted.

"Might I be of some help to ya, laddie?" a middle-aged woman asked. Her curly hair was the exact same color as Bozo the Clown.

"I was looking for a place where I could practice piano," I told her.

She studied me closely. "Ya sound like an American."

I nodded, then smiled. "Yes, that's right. My mother and I came to Ireland for Christmas."

She smiled back at me now. "Well, I s'pose 'twouldn't hurt to let ya play a bit. Since there's no one much about." She nodded over her shoulder. "'Ceptin' for the old lads having their stout, and I doubt they'll pay you much mind. Just keep it down, though."

"Thanks."

I waited for her to leave before I slowly approached the piano. I knew that Ireland was a damp climate; hopefully this piano was in tune. I ran my fingers over the smooth wooden surface of the wood, then sat down, almost reverently, on the padded seat. Then, after stretching my fingers a little, I started to play. It felt so good to feel the ivory keys beneath my fingers again. To start with, I played the piece I'd been working on at home, back in the warehouse. Then I did some variations on it, giving it what I liked to think was an Irish flare, and it really seemed to work. I played for about an hour before the orange-haired woman returned. To my surprise, she started to clap when I finished my final song.

"That was absolutely lovely," she said. "Ya come on up here and play anytime ya like. Bring your mother too."

Now that gave me an idea. "Could I make a reservation for dinner tonight?" I asked eagerly. "For my mother and me?"

"'Twould be my pleasure," she said.

So I gave her my name and told her we'd be there around seven.

"Jamie Frederick," she said, sticking out her hand to shake mine. "'Tis a delight to make your acquaintance. And I am Kerry McVee, and ta sole proprietress of the Anchor Inn, left to me by my late husband Bobby, God bless his soul."

"Pleased to meet you, Mrs. McVee."

"Just call me Kerry." She smiled. "So I'll be seeing you and your mother at seven then?"

"And would it be okay if I played the piano tonight? Maybe just a song or two?"

"Ya can play the whole night long if ya like, laddie. If it were my busy season, I'd even offer to pay ya for your music. Unfortunately, 'tis the slow time o' year and I'm barely able to make ends meet."

"That's okay. I don't want to be paid." Then, excited about my spur-of-the-moment plan, I decided to let her in on it. "You see, my mother doesn't even know that I can play piano. This will be her first time to hear me."

"She doesn't know?"

I shook my head. "She knows that I play guitar, but I took up piano a couple of years ago, and I never told her."

"Isn't she in for a lucky surprise."

"Yes," I agreed. "So I'd appreciate it if you didn't say anything."

"Mum's the word." She put a forefinger over her lips and winked. "And I won't mention it to your mum either."

I hoped that would be the case as I retraced my steps back to town, making it to the hotel just as it was getting dusky. I wasn't sure if Mom was back yet, but just in case she was resting or immersed in a new book, I decided not to disturb her. I wrote a note on the hotel stationery, telling her about the reservations for dinner at the Anchor Inn, then slipped it beneath her door.

My plan was to play for her, maybe between dinner and dessert, giving us both time to relax and enjoy the evening. And then, after playing, I would lay my cards on the table and tell her the truth about dropping out of college. I knew this would be a tough conversation. And in some ways, I'd just as soon avoid it altogether. But I also knew that music was a huge part of my life, and I didn't want to hide it any longer. Besides, I had several things working in my favor. First, I would be breaking this news in a public place so that Mom wouldn't be able to get too angry since she never did like to make a scene; and second, Mom and I had been getting along better than ever these past couple of days and her sympathy levels should be good; and finally, Mom actually liked good music and hopefully she'd be proud of what I'd done and this new direction I'd taken. At least that's what I hoped. It seemed to make perfect sense.

Even so, I was incredibly nervous as I waited for Mom to join me in the hotel lobby. I hadn't been this uptight since

Jamie and the Muskrats had made our debut at a high school fall formal back in '61. I nervously stood near the stairs, pretending to study the small rack of tourism information while I waited. I even stuck one of the fishing excursion pamphlets into my pocket. I'd already asked the desk clerk to call a cab for us since I knew that it would be too far for Mom to walk, plus it was dark out now anyway. He told me there weren't any cabs in Clifden, but that he could get us a Hackney car. I wasn't sure what that meant, but if he thought it would do the trick, it was fine by me.

I'd even dressed carefully, putting on the new tweed jacket that Mom had gotten for me, along with a clean white shirt and a striped tie. I wasn't too sure about the stripes with the tweed, but I'd only brought along a couple of ties and this one seemed to work the best.

"Jamie," Mom said as she emerged from the geriatric elevator. "Don't you look handsome."

I grinned at her. "You look nice too." Mom had on her blue suit, complete with matching hat and gloves. I think that suit was made by some famous designer with a name like Coco Puffs or something I could never quite remember. But Dad had always liked how it brought out the color of her eyes.

I held the door for my mom. "I think our Hackney car is out here."

"What?" she asked curiously.

So I explained about the cab situation and where we were going. "This place has an amazing view of the ocean in the daytime, and the lady who runs it is really nice," I told her as I helped her into the car.

"How did you find out about it?"

"Just asked around," I said casually.

The wind was picking up a little as we went up the walk toward the restaurant. "I hope our good weather isn't about to blow away," Mom said as she kept her round, little blue hat from going airborne. "It was so nice out this afternoon."

The Anchor Inn was well lit inside, complete with a crackling fire in the big rock fireplace. I noticed now that there were even sprigs of holly about, hanging over pictures and across the mantel. A nice bit of Christmas cheer, understated but charming. Mom should like that. Also, there were candles lit, one in each windowsill. A nice touch and great atmosphere. And there, just as it had been earlier today, sat the grand piano, the dark wood gleaming as if it had just been polished, almost as if it were waiting for me.

"Welcome," Kerry said as I introduced my mother. "I hope you're enjoying your visit in Ireland."

"We're both falling in love with your beautiful country," Mom said as Kerry led us to a table not far from the piano. There were a couple of other parties here tonight, but most of the tables were vacant, and I could understand the concerns about lack of business. It was a wonder the place even stayed open.

Kerry smiled brightly. "That's what we like to hear from our neighbors across the sea. One day we hope to have a bustling tourist trade here in Ireland."

Dinner turned out to be very good, and despite the high prices Mom seemed completely pleased with my choice of restaurants. Our quiet but attentive waiter, Dolan, introduced himself as Kerry's younger brother. But other than that bit of info and bringing us our food and drinks, he kept to himself.

"Dessert?" he asked as he cleared our dinner plates.

"Sure," I said quickly, worried that Mom might try to get the check before I had a chance to do my mini concert. "What do you have?"

Dolan went over a short list, and Mom chose the custard and I went with chocolate cake. Then I excused myself to "the men's room." And I actually did go to the men's room, but it was only to take some deep breaths and to calm myself. Then I went out, walked straight to the piano, and sat down. I was within plain sight of my mother, but she wasn't looking that way, which was just fine. It gave me another moment to compose myself and to focus. And then I began to play, glancing at Mom but focusing on the music.

To begin with, she didn't even look my way. She appeared completely absorbed by her cup of tea. And then quickly, almost as if she'd heard a gunshot, she turned around and just stared at me with wide eyes. I couldn't quite read her expression. It seemed a mixture of astonishment and horror, which really made no sense. Good grief, it wasn't like I was dancing on a table; I was simply playing the piano. Feeling even less at ease, I diverted my eyes but continued to play. When I finished my first piece, the small group of diners actually clapped. Even my mother clapped, although I could tell by the mechanical way that she moved her hands back and forth like a stiff marionette that she was still in some kind of shock. So I decided to play another piece. Then another. I suppose it was a delay technique, buying myself enough time in the hope that the next phase of my little dinner show might proceed a bit more smoothly. Finally, I stood up after the fourth piece. Once again I was pleased to hear the applause, even more enthusiastic than before. Even Kerry and Dolan and workers from the kitchen were clapping.

"Well . . . ," my mom said when I rejoined her.

"Well?" I studied her face. It seemed unreasonably pale, and I couldn't figure why she was reacting like this. My intention had been to please her with my musical skill. It was no secret that my mother enjoyed music, particularly piano, although her leanings were more to classical and light jazz. But I had hoped to gain her approval with my performance and then to gently break the news about what I'd been up to these past couple of years. It had seemed the perfect ploy.

But she just slowly shook her head, and her brow creased as if she were deeply troubled about something. She kept twisting the linen napkin between her fingers, something she often told me not to do, and her untouched dessert was pushed away to the side. "Wherever did you learn to play *like that*?"

Now it's possible that she didn't mean those words to come out the way that they sounded to me, but it was hard not to feel just a little offended. "Like *what*?" I said crisply, suddenly on the defensive.

She waved her hands, as if searching for words. "Well, it's a different sort of style," she said carefully, as if weighing each word. "Not the sort of thing one hears every day."

"So, you didn't like it?" I demanded.

"No . . . that's not it, Jamie." Her eyes looked slightly misty now. "I just wondered where you'd learned to play like that. That's all. One might think you'd taken music classes somewhere."

The time had come. I knew I might as well get this over with as quickly and painlessly as possible. If she took it badly, there wasn't much I could do. I cleared my throat. "There's something I need to tell you, Mom."

9

Colleen

I stared at Jamie as if staring at a complete stranger. How had this happened? What was the meaning? The whole thing was unsettling, disturbing, eerily haunting even—almost like seeing a ghost. Yes, that was exactly what it was like! It was as if I'd seen the ghost of Liam O'Neil just now, sitting there at the piano and playing like *that*. Of course, Jamie had no idea why my reaction to his music was so irrational, so unlike me. And, while I felt badly for catching him off guard and putting him on the defensive, I also felt that I was maintaining rather well not to have fallen out of my chair.

"There's something I need to tell you," he was saying and I was attempting to focus, but at the same time thinking, *No, Jamie, there's something I need to tell you.* Still he continued, the words poured out quickly, in the form of a confession of sorts.

"I didn't graduate from business college," he said. "I used the money that Dad sent to take some music classes at

Berkeley. Then I quit school completely, supporting myself and my band with the tuition money while I seriously pursued music. I had meant to tell you guys. But then Dad died and I didn't want to upset you. And time passed and the lie just kept going."

"You didn't graduate?" I said, trying to absorb this new fact. Perhaps even using it as a distraction from the emotions that were raging through me—memories of Liam and how he once played like that.

He nodded. "I'm sorry, Mom. I know I should've told you. But there just didn't seem to be the right opportunity." Then he smiled, that same little half smile that he'd used on me since he was a toddler. "But I *love* music. It's all I want to do and—"

"How long had you been lying about school, Jamie?" I knew my words sounded harsh, and much colder than I meant them to be, but it was as if all my emotions had risen to the surface, hammering to get out, and I didn't even know where to begin. Focusing on Jamie seemed the easiest route.

"It was winter term in '61 that I quit."

"And you kept this a secret the whole time?" I frowned as I considered how this would have hurt Hal. "You never told your father?"

"I tried to once, Mom. But he was so insistent that I'd take over the shoe store. All he wanted was for me to get my business degree and start selling shoes. I didn't want—"

"But you continued taking his money?" I stared at my son, seeing how much he looked like his birth father, and feeling shocked by this. But I made myself believe that my shock was because he had deceived us and that we had never even suspected. "That whole time you kept taking his money and pretending that you were going to school? What else were you keeping from us?" I could hear the venom in my voice, and yet I felt helpless.

He pressed his lips tightly together, as if he were biting his tongue, holding back the words he probably wanted to say. And his hands were curling into fists, as if he wanted to pound them on the table, to make his point. Instead, he just stood. "I know you're angry, Mom. And I don't blame you for that, but somehow I thought—" He looked longingly at the piano now. "I thought that maybe if you understood how much I love—" Then his voice broke.

"I'm sorry," he said then turned and walked away. Heading straight for the big carved door, he slowly opened it and, without looking back, walked out.

Suddenly my anger seemed foolish . . . and, in some ways, even selfish. And now I felt desperate. My son had laid his heart on the table, confessed to his deception, and I had treated him like a criminal. I knew I had hurt Jamie deeply, and I didn't know what to do next. I glanced around the quiet dining room, curious as to whether or not we'd made a spectacle, and yet not really caring either. But the other diners seemed fine, as if they hadn't noticed a thing. Or perhaps they were simply being polite.

"Everything all right?" asked the owner, the woman with bright orangey-red hair that had to have come out of a bottle. I couldn't remember her name.

"I, uh, I'm not sure," I admitted. "I think I'd like the bill, please."

Then she left, I assumed to tell Dolan to bring the bill, but a few minutes later, she was the one who returned. With the bill in her hand, she sat down across from me, the same spot where Jamie should've been sitting right now.

"Jamie's a fine musician," she said. "'Tis a boy 'twould make any mother proud."

I blinked in surprise. Who was this woman and how did she know my son? I simply nodded. "Yes. He's always been a good boy."

"But you're unhappy with him now."

"I'm frustrated," I admitted, still wondering who she was and why she felt the need to intrude into my personal affairs. "We had a little misunderstanding."

"About his piano playing?"

I glanced over to the door, curious as to whether he'd come back or not. Maybe he was just taking a little stroll, to cool off. Maybe the right thing to do was to wait for him to come back.

"Jamie told me that ya did not know—'twas meant to be a surprise."

I stared at this strange woman. Just how much did she know anyway? "I'm sorry," I said, "but I totally forgot your name."

She smiled. "Kerry. Kerry McVee."

I swallowed hard. "Kerry, you seem like a nice person. And I'm not sure how much Jamie told you. But . . ." I paused then shook my head. "Let's just say this is a little bit complicated."

"Yes, the best things in life usually are." She waved at her brother who had just given another table their bill. "Dolan," she called. "Bring us a fresh pot of tea, will ya?" Then she turned back to me and smiled with warm eyes. "Why don't ya tell me all about it?"

I felt my eyes getting moist now. I wasn't sure if it was due to her unexpected kindness or the tumultuous emotions I'd just experienced with Jamie and the piano, but I felt as if a thick wall inside of me was crumbling. The dam that had held back my secret for so long was about to break. I knew it was time to open up, and Kerry seemed a safe person to confide in. "It's a long story . . ."

She nodded. "I have time." Then she glanced at the door too. "Let's just talk until he comes back."

"*If* he comes back . . ."

"He's a grown lad, dear. And a smart one too. He'll be all right."

So I took in a deep breath and I began. "I was so shocked when Jamie started to play the piano. I had no idea that he knew how to play, that he had any interest in it. I mean, he'd gotten a guitar in high school, like so many boys who wanted to be the next Buddy Holly. And he and some of his friends would play out in the garage. Mostly that loud crazy music that I can't stand. I just figured it was a phase."

"But perhaps 'tis something more?"

"Yes. You see, Jamie's father was a musician too. Oh, Jamie doesn't know this. In fact, he doesn't even know who his *real* father is—" I took in a sharp breath, shocked that I'd just made this confession.

"Go on, Colleen. This is not a new story, you must know that."

"No, I suppose it's not." I gathered my thoughts, turning back the clock, back to twenty-two years earlier, back to the fall of 1941. "I had moved to Hollywood, from a farm in the Midwest," I began. "I thought I was going to become a movie star." I laughed and told her a bit about my high school acting days. "Of course, that did not prepare me for Hollywood in the least. Although I did manage to get a few small jobs, a couple of photo shoots for soap advertisements along with some runway modeling. But after two years, it wasn't really working out like I'd planned. It was a week before Thanksgiving, and I had actually considered giving the whole acting thing up and going home for good. You know it was wartime and several of my brothers had been shipped off to Europe and I knew my family missed me. But my roommate Wanda, who was also trying to get her big Hollywood break, talked me into going to a party with her. She thought we might make some good connections, meet somebody important, a director or producer, someone who could change our lives." I remembered everything about that night. How Wanda and I had both dressed carefully, how we split the cab fare, knowing we'd be broke tomorrow, both hoping this could be it—our big night.

"And did you meet someone important?"

"Oh, I'll admit there were some impressive people at that party. And, yes, I did meet someone who changed my life . . ." I remember the crowded room now, seeing the handsome man at the piano, the way his head bent ever so slightly as he played, just the way my son's had done tonight. He was a friend of the host's, just playing for the fun of it. "But not in the way I had planned." I sighed, remembering the way I felt when he picked me out of the crowd, the way he spoke to me as if he really knew me, knew everything about me, and later the way he touched my face, our first kiss. A delightful shiver ran down my spine just to remember the feel of his touch, how my heart raced when we danced, when he held me close. It was like nothing I'd ever experienced before . . . or since.

Kerry smiled. "And you fell in love?"

"Is it that obvious?"

"Your cheeks are flushed."

I touched my face. "Oh . . ."

"It's lovely."

I took in another deep breath, trying to decide how much more to say to her. And yet it felt good to finally tell this to someone—like a confession, wasn't it supposed to be good for the soul? Especially if I could tell someone who I would, in all likelihood, never have to see again. "I'd never been with a man," I admitted. "I was saving myself for marriage. But something happened when I was with him—something wild and uncontrollable. We spent the next three days together, and I felt as if I would follow that man anywhere . . . I'd do anything to be with him forever. Do you know what I mean?"

She had a wistful expression now. "It's been many years ago, but I do remember that feeling. So, what happened?"

"He was an officer in the Navy, a communications specialist, and was being shipped to Honolulu. Pearl Harbor."

Her pale brows arched. "Oh . . ."

"Yes. It was 1941 and he shipped off a few days before Thanksgiving. He was due to arrive the third of December.

But before he left, he asked me to marry him. He told me he loved me and he wanted us to go down to city hall and do it right then and there, but I wanted to wait . . ." I bit my lip and for the millionth time asked myself why—why didn't I agree to marry him that day?

"So, you didn't marry?"

"No. I wanted to plan a small wedding. I wanted some of my family to come out and meet him. He was so wonderful, I knew they'd all love him. And Liam didn't think he'd be in Honolulu more than a couple of weeks. He felt certain he'd be back for Christmas."

"Liam?" she said with interest. "Was he Irish by chance?"

I nodded eagerly. "Yes! Rather, his parents had been—they had immigrated before he was born. But it had always been his dream to come to Ireland someday. That was why I wanted to come here now, and why I brought my son. I thought it would be a good place to tell him . . . the truth."

"So am I correct to assume that Liam died in the bombing of Pearl Harbor?"

I swallowed hard, then nodded. "Because we weren't married . . . I was never notified of his death . . . but all my letters were returned. I searched the Red Cross lists, but I'd heard that many names hadn't been included yet. But then I never heard a word from him either."

Kerry reached over and put her hand on mine. "And you were with child."

"Yes . . . and I knew that Liam had been going over there to work on the Arizona," I said. "So many were killed . . . I knew in my heart that he was gone."

"What did you do?"

"I considered going home and lying to my parents, telling them that I'd been briefly married, then widowed, and I could almost convince myself that it was true. And I wanted to stay in California, in case he came back. But while I was waiting, hoping to hear from Liam, Wanda got married, and I couldn't afford the apartment. So I took a job at a shoe store in a nearby town and rented a room there. I knew my Hollywood dreams were finished by then."

"Not much call for actresses with a bulging belly, I'll venture."

I shook my head. "The man I worked for, the owner of the shoe store, was so kind and generous to me. He was the one who helped me find a room to rent. Although it didn't take him long to figure things out. I tried to cover it up, but I began to show in the spring. Plus I had morning sickness for nearly half of the pregnancy. One day, when I'd been late for work again, he called me into his office and I just knew that he was going to fire me. But, instead, he proposed."

"And you accepted."

"I didn't know what else to do. I told Hal the truth, the complete truth. He said it didn't matter and that we would raise the child as our own. The only thing he asked of me was to never speak of it again. So I didn't."

"Until now."

"Yes. He died a year and a half ago."

"I'm sorry."

"So am I. But I feel that Jamie needs to know the truth. Perhaps more than ever after hearing him tonight. He is his father's son."

"'Tis amazing . . . a son would play music like the father, and yet they never met." She just shook her head.

The dining room was quiet now. All the other diners had left, and I suddenly realized it was getting quite late. "I should be going," I said, standing and opening my purse. "I'm worried about Jamie. I should check on him." I reached for the bill.

But Kerry got it before I could and she crumpled it up in her hand. "Dinner is on the house tonight."

"No," I insisted. "You must let me pay."

She gave me a stern look. "You need to respect Irish hospitality, Colleen. If I say you're my guest for dinner, ya should not argue with me."

"May I leave a tip?"

She smiled. "Certainly."

I slipped what I hoped would be a generous tip beneath my teacup and thanked her.

"Do come again," she said. "And bring Jamie along. I would love to hear the lad play some more of that lovely music. He has a gift, you know, a real gift."

I forced a smile, unsure if I'd ever be able to talk my son into playing anything again. At least not for me. "I'll tell him you said that."

"Or if you'd like to come on up here for a spot of tea," she said hopefully. "Please, drop by. We have a lovely view in the daytime and I make some scones that are renown in the region."

"Yes," I said suddenly. "I'd like that. Thank you!"

10

Jamie

I didn't know how things had gone so crooked for me tonight. Everything had seemed just about perfect, and then—bam—it all went sideways. I was walking back toward town, trying to find my way in the dark, and wondering why there weren't more streetlamps out here. Although, to be fair, I was still a ways from town. I could hear the sound of the ocean to my right, the waves smashing onto the rocks in a lonely way, a way that made me long for something . . . something I couldn't even put my finger on.

Finally—feeling like, what was the use, why try to figure it out?—I found a boulder planted next to the gravel road and just sat down on it. I could see some sort of light off in the distance, and to my surprise it turned out to be the moon, rising up over the sea. I watched with fascination as it came over the surface of the ocean, reflecting a long, cool slice of blue light over the water. It wasn't a full moon, but it was getting close. Maybe three-quarters or seven-eighths. I'd never been great at geometry.

Like an LP record with a deep scratch, I kept replaying Mom's reaction to my confession tonight, trying to understand where it had gone wrong, and why. Why hadn't I been able to use the music and some of the charm I've been accused of misusing to bring this whole thing around and make her understand that my choices had really been for the best in the end? Why had she gotten so upset? I knew that no parents want to be deceived, but sometimes it just happened. To be fair, it had happened all my life. Mom was well aware that her son was no angel. But she'd always forgiven me before. I usually got off pretty easily too—even my friends thought I was a little spoiled. And yet, my mother just didn't seem like herself tonight. As if she'd been caught off guard, she'd seemed so shocked, so taken aback, and so unlike her usual cool, calm, and well-mannered self. Looking back, it was just plain weird.

I picked up a stone and chucked it out as far as I could, trying to make it to the sea, but hearing no splash. I thought about my dad, wondering how he would've reacted to all this, and I honestly felt like he might've taken it better. Sure, he would've been shocked at first, but then he would've listened, he would've tried to see my side. Despite the fact that he'd always wanted me to go into the shoe business, that he'd never thought music could ever provide a means to live, but something a guy ought to do just for the fun of it, I still think he would've understood me eventually. Oh, he would've been disappointed in me for lying to him. No doubt about that. Especially since Dad lived by a strict code of ethics, a code that was ruled by his faith in God. But he would've gotten over it. And because of his faith, he would've forgiven me too. I knew that for a fact. Plus he probably would've forgiven me a whole lot quicker than Mom, that was assuming that she ever would. Man, I wished I had told the truth sooner, back when Dad was still alive. I thought about that old saying about weaving tangled webs by telling lies. It seemed to be true.

I didn't know how long I'd been sitting there, but I finally decided that I was cold and I should probably get back to the hotel. I knew that Mom would be worried about me, but I thought maybe that was a good thing. Maybe she'd have time to think and maybe even feel bad about her reaction. It seemed the least she could've done was to compliment me on learning to play piano. Even if she didn't like the style or whatever it was that seemed to displease her. Who could figure out mothers these days? That reminded me of her main purpose in bringing me to Ireland. How could I have forgotten? Oh, she hadn't really spoken of it lately and I was sure if I confronted her now, she'd deny it. But I had no doubt that her plan was to talk me out of joining the Air Force while we were here. I knew that she wanted to keep me home, and I suspected she thought if she kept me on a tight leash, playing the handyman around her house, that I would be safe and sound.

Well, my mother still had a few lessons to learn. As far as joining the Air Force went, I was more committed to it now than ever before. The first thing I'd do once we got back home would be to go sign up. And I knew they'd take me too. I'd done sports throughout high school and for fun afterward, so I was in pretty good shape. Plus nearly two full years of business college wouldn't hurt either. Hopefully it'd get me a better status once I enlisted, maybe even an officer. I'd have to look into that.

So, as I stood up and started walking toward town, it was with a new authority. I was going to join the Air Force. I might even become a pilot. And eventually, like it or not, my mother would learn to respect me for it.

Once I got to town, I decided I wasn't ready to face Mom quite yet. It wasn't even ten, and I suspected that she'd still be up. Probably waiting for me. So I went into the pub where the live music was playing, and although this band wasn't as good as the one in Dublin, probably because they were older and maybe a little more traditional, they were still good. Very good. And I enjoyed listening to them. I decided to stick around until the place closed up. That way I could probably avoid seeing my mother altogether tonight. And even if it made her worry a little, I didn't see how that could hurt. As I drank my second pint of stout, I wondered if my mother had any idea of how deeply she had hurt my feelings tonight. Or if she even cared.

11

Colleen

I tossed and turned until after midnight, worried sick about Jamie, but hoping he was all right and that I hadn't hurt him too badly. Although I knew I had. Oh, I'm sure he expected me to be upset, but normally, we would discuss such things in a civilized way if we were in public. I knew I'd have to explain myself. Jamie had no idea that I was reacting more to his music and my memories of Liam than I was to the news that he dropped out of college. In fact, I think I suspected he hadn't graduated. My own sister had suggested as much. Somehow I needed to make him understand. I needed to tell him the truth . . . perhaps even tomorrow.

Finally when it was nearly one, I heard footsteps down the hallway and then a key turning in the door next to mine, and I knew he'd made it back safely.

Still, it was hard to shut down my mind. So many old and new feelings tumbled inside my head; like my old Whirlpool washer when it got stuck on the spin cycle, things just kept spinning round and round. Would I ever be able to sort it all out? And how was I going to explain it all to Jamie? Telling my story to Kerry tonight had been a relief of sorts, but at the same time it had stirred up the pot, a pot that I'd managed to keep quiet for a long time. Now I was plagued with old questions, haunted by forgotten longings, and even obsessing over that old *what might have been*. . . . What if things had gone differently? What if I'd said *yes* to Liam, instead of *wait*?

But I'd been through all that before . . . so long ago that it seemed like another person, another lifetime. At the time I'd picked up the only survival skill that seemed to work—I learned to move on. I learned to focus my emotions and energies on the task at hand, whether it was having a baby, being a new mom, helping to sell shoes, or volunteering in the community. I simply moved on.

But I felt blindsided by this misunderstanding with Jamie—without even making my disclosure, our relationship had already hit the rocks. What if things got worse? What if I lost him completely? I wasn't sure I could survive that. Maybe I needed to rethink my plan. Maybe I was being too hasty.

Suddenly I wondered why I'd ever felt the need to tell him about his birth father in the first place. What difference did it really make? What was done was done. Nothing I could say or do would change the past. Why not let sleeping dogs lie? Then I remembered how he'd announced his intention to join the Air Force, and the chill of fear that had rushed through me when I imagined him going to war. It seemed just my luck that Jamie wanted to follow in his birth father's footsteps—whether he knew about him or not.

Hadn't his style of music been a clear sign of that tonight? I was stunned to hear him playing—so like Liam that it was eerie. And, for one brief, crazy moment, I thought I'd gone back into time. I thought that Liam was still alive, still young and handsome, still playing the piano. It was as if Pearl Harbor had never happened. And then I actually pinched myself, realizing it wasn't Liam, it was *my* son. And Liam's son. So strange.

And who could tell with fate? Perhaps the son was designed to be a shadow of the father, something predisposed even before his birth. What if my attempts to intervene made no difference? What would be, would simply be. *Que será, será*. Why try to fight what seemed written in stone, or perhaps in the stars? What if God's cosmic sense of humor was cynical? Maybe he got a kick out of watching history repeating itself. My dear Liam had played the piano, gone off to war, and died. In all likelihood Jamie would do the same. I callously wondered if Jamie might even get a girl pregnant before he trucked off to war and an early grave.

Finally I told my mind to *be quiet*—to just *shut up*! Quit dwelling on all that was negative and pessimistic and frightening . . . I reminded myself of what Hal had often said, whenever I was fretting over Jamie or life in general. He'd quietly put his hand on my shoulder and say, "Why work yourself into a fit over things you can't control, Colleen? Why not simply pray?"

Maybe he had been right. Perhaps prayer was my only ally now. And so I did pray. But first I had to apologize for imagining God as some heartless practical joker. I had a feeling that wasn't quite right. Then I prayed for help and mercy and wisdom. And then I fell into a fretful sleep and dreamed some crazy, mixed-up dreams involving Liam, Hal, and Jamie.

The next morning, I got up early, but I was not refreshed. I didn't feel the least bit rested or peaceful, and I wasn't even happy about being here in Ireland. Doubtful thoughts clouded my head as I pulled on my quilted bathrobe and opened the curtains. It was still dark out, but the sky looked as if it might be clear again today, and I could see a sliver of golden light off to the southeastern horizon, out over the ocean. It seemed likely that we could have another nice day, not that I cared since I felt certain another storm brewed, one between Jamie and me. Yet, I knew what had to be done. I knew I must place one foot in front of the other, and I must speak to my son, and somehow I must make amends. I would take the high road and apologize for how things went last night. I would forgive him for his wasted college money and his deceptions, and I would tell him that we needed a fresh start.

But would I tell him the truth about his father? I still felt unsure. Was it best to just get these things out in the open, to lay my cards on the table and see what happened next? Or was it wrong to burden him with my mistakes? It was too early to figure that out. Instead, I slowly bathed, then dressed, shivering in the cool air of the bathroom and wondering why the Irish hadn't discovered the lovely convenience of bathroom wall heaters.

Then I busied myself in my room until 7:30, and although I knew it was still pretty early for Jamie, I went out and tapped on his door. When there was no answer, I tapped a bit louder. Surely he hadn't gotten up and left already. I hadn't heard a peep from his room since last night. And he'd come in so late. I knocked even louder now, calling out his name, and eventually I heard some thumping around, and he opened the door, blinked sleepily at me, and asked me what time it was.

"It's after 7:30," I told him. "I was going down for breakfast and wondered if you'd like to join me. I think we should talk."

"Give me a few minutes," he said groggily as he closed the door. "Gotta wake up and stuff."

This seemed reasonable, so I got my new book, an Irish novel set in the eighteenth century, and went down to the lobby to read for a while. Then, when it was a quarter past eight, I went on into the dining room. I figured forty-five minutes was plenty of time for Jamie to clean up. I knew that, if in a hurry, like back in high school and he had slept in too late, that boy could be out the door in five minutes flat.

I ordered a pot of tea. But after another fifteen minutes, with no Jamie, I went ahead and ordered my breakfast.

"My son seems to be running late," I told the waitress as she brought me my bacon and eggs. Then, although I ate slowly, glancing every now and then to the door, I was finally finished with my meal, and the only thing left to do was to sign for the bill and go back upstairs to see what was keeping Jamie. I hoped he hadn't sneaked out on me. It was nine o'clock when I knocked on the door again and after a couple of minutes, Jamie answered, looking exactly as he had the first time.

"I waited for you," I told him in a slightly irritated tone. "For an hour and a half."

He yawned. "I must've fallen back asleep."

I studied his red-rimmed and slightly puffy eyes, then remembered he'd had a late night, which made me suspicious. "Were you out drinking last night?" I demanded.

"I had a couple of pints, no big deal." He frowned.

"Look, I didn't bring you all the way over to Ireland just so you could go on a drunken binge every night." I instantly regretted my words, aware that my voice sounded just like an old fishwife. But it was too late; like a gun that had been shot, my bullet words were out and they had hit their mark.

"I haven't been on any *drunken binges*, Mom." He was closing the door now.

"I heard you coming in after one in the morning." I wedged my foot in the door, keeping it open. Part of my brain warned me to be the grown-up here, to talk reasonably and make peace, but the other part was putting up its fists, ready to go the next round.

"I was listening to a band."

"After midnight?"

"What is this?" he shot back at me, eyes narrowed. "The Irish inquisition?"

"Well, *I'm your mother*, Jamie. And I brought you here to—"

"Yes, you are my mother," he said loudly. "Although I doubt that anyone would've known that last night when you raked me over the coals and didn't even acknowledge my music. What kind of mother does that anyway?"

I pushed open the door now, worried that our voices might be disturbing other hotel guests, not that there were many this time of year. Still, this was uncomfortable—and embarrassing.

"We need to talk, Jamie," I said firmly as I went into his room and closed the door. I stood before him with my hands on my hips, just the way I had done so many times while he was growing up, times when he had to be nagged to clean his room, or to finish his homework, or to undo some childish prank. More than Hal, I had been the disciplinarian with my son, and it seemed I wasn't ready to give up my role yet.

"Sit down," I commanded him, pointing to his unmade bed. To my surprise he did this without arguing, and I sat on the chair across from him.

He perched on the edge of his bed just staring at me, but I could see the hurt in his deep blue eyes, and I knew I was the one responsible for it. And I knew why. But I wasn't sure I wanted to face that just yet.

Suddenly it occurred to me that I was coming at this thing completely backward. After all, he'd been the one to make that shocking confession last night. I still couldn't believe how casually he had lied to both Hal and me, pretending to go to college when he'd been wasting our money and just playing around. For two years he'd kept up this deception. What made him think it was acceptable to take our money, abuse our trust, and then lie about graduating? We hadn't brought him up to be like that, and I had every right to be indignant and angry. And yet . . . was I using these emotions for a smoke screen?

"Just say it, Mom," he said, breaking into my internal battlefield. "Tell me that you're ashamed of me, that I'm a good-for-nothing son, that I'm useless and hopeless, and that I stole the tuition money from you. Just say it. I know that's what you're thinking."

I blinked, then took in a sharp breath. "Yes, I *am* disappointed in you, Jamie." I reminded myself I had meant to be in control here. I had planned to be mature, whether or not I felt like it. I wondered how Hal would handle this. Probably much better than I was doing. "I really did want you to go to college, and I wanted you to graduate too. I thought a college degree would be your ticket, your way to get a solid heads-up in life, a key to success. And I wanted it even more after you decided not to go into the family business. I can't deny that it hurt me to hear that you'd deceived us, Jamie. I think it would've hurt your father too."

"Yeah, I know, Mom." He held up his hands in a helpless gesture. "But at least Dad would've forgiven me."

Now that stung. "I'll forgive you too, Jamie."

He scowled. "Yeah, maybe you'll forgive me, but not until you get good and ready. Not until you've punished me first."

"I don't *want* to punish you," I said. "I just want you to understand how I feel. You used your father's money . . . pretending to go to school . . . you took advantage of him, Jamie. And he's not even here to defend him—"

"Are you trying to lay some big guilt trip on me? Maybe you really do think it's my fault that Dad had a heart attack. And he's not here to set us straight."

"No . . . no, that's not it." I felt lost now. I was saying things that really didn't matter, going down rabbit trails that had nothing to do with why I brought Jamie to Ireland in the first place, or what I felt I needed to tell him. I leaned over and placed my head in my hands, trying to figure it out. What was I supposed to do here?

"Then what do you want, Mom? You want me to get a job and pay you back that money? Would that make it better? I can do that if that's what it'll take to—"

"No, Jamie," I said, sitting up and looking at him, preparing myself for what I knew I had to do. "It's really *not* about the money."

"It's just that I'm a loser, isn't it? That I dropped out of college, and now you'll have to tell all your friends that I'm just a—"

"Jamie, that's not it!"

"*Well, what is it, Mom?* What is making you act like such a weirdo? Why are you making such a humongous deal out of something that's over and done with—something I can't change even if I wanted to? I told you that I'm sorry. And I can work to pay you back, if that's what it takes."

"That's not—"

"And I don't know why you're so opposed to my music. It's not even rock and roll. Man, I actually thought you would like it." His eyes glistened as he stared at me, looking like a lost and confused boy now. "I cannot believe that I actually thought that you would like it!" He picked up his pillow and slammed a fist into it. "What a complete dope I've been. About everything."

"I *did* like it, Jamie," I spoke quietly now, measuring my words, trying to gauge if this was really the right time or not. I had imagined it happening so differently. I'd planned to tell him when we were doing something fun, perhaps on a ferryboat ride, or driving through the countryside, or enjoying a nice meal. Not like this. Not with him still wearing his rumpled pajamas, sitting here in his messy hotel room, punching his pillow like an eight-year-old. I hadn't imagined myself feeling this close to the edge, sitting here with clenched fists and on the verge of tears. This was all wrong. But maybe that didn't matter.

"So why did you act like that?" he demanded. "Like you thought it was so weird when I played the piano, as if my music made you miserable and that you'd just as soon never hear me play again? *Why, Mom?*"

"Because . . ." I took a deep breath. "It was the *way* you played the piano last night, Jamie." The words were coming out so slowly, one at a time in a mechanical way, as if someone else was doing the talking for me, like one of those new "chatty" dolls—you pulled the string and out came the words. "It was the style that you played, Jamie . . . it sounded exactly the same as . . . well, it was the same *way* that your father used to play . . . and when I heard it I was shocked and it felt as if someone had punched me in the stomach or pulled the rug out from under me . . . I felt confused and upset and I just didn't know how to deal with it and consequently I reacted poorly."

Jamie just sat there with the most confused expression. I knew he was trying to put this together, to make sense of my completely senseless confession.

"Huh?" His head actually cocked to one side, like a bewildered puppy. "I didn't know Dad played the piano."

"Yes, that's right. Your dad, I mean Hal, *didn't* play the piano . . ."

"But you just said—"

"Your *father* played the piano, Jamie." I took in a deep breath, bracing myself. "Your *father*, a man you never met, a man named Liam O'Neil, played the piano—in almost the exact same way that you played it last night, Jamie. And it was just too much for me to deal with at the time."

Jamie's eyes were huge now. "What are you saying?"

"I'm trying to tell you something," I continued. "It's not easy, and it's a big part of the reason that I brought you to Ireland in the first place. Hal Frederick was not your *real* father. Certainly, he was your *dad*, Jamie. And he was a fine dad. But your real father, your *birth* father, was Liam O'Neil."

Jamie shook his head as if he was trying to get water out of his ears. "*What?*"

"I know you must be shocked by this," I said calmly. "Probably similar to the way I felt last night, only far more so."

"Shocked?" He stood up now. "Shocked doesn't even begin to describe it. What exactly are you saying here, Mom?"

So for the second time in twenty-four hours, I told my story. Only this time I edited a few things, telling the story in the way that a mother would want her only son to hear it. "I was young and foolish and in love," I finally admitted. "Liam did ask me to marry him, but I had no idea I was, uh, with child. And being young and foolish, I wanted to have a real wedding, so I told your father that I'd wait for him to come back. He was only supposed to be in Hawaii for a few weeks, working out some communications problems on a battleship. But he arrived just a few days before Pearl Harbor . . . and he never made it back."

"My *real* father died in Pearl Harbor?" Jamie was pacing across the room now, running his hand through his already messy hair. "My *real* father was a stranger named Liam—what was his last name again?"

"O'Neil."

"Was he Irish?"

"His parents were Irish; they had immigrated before he was born. Liam grew up in the Boston area. He'd gone to Annapolis and was an officer in the Navy when we met."

"A military man?"

"Yes, one who was killed in a battle where they never even got to fight back."

Jamie was still pacing, shaking his head as he tried to absorb all of this, trying to make heads or tales of my crazy mess. I felt sorry for him. It was a heavy load for a young man to carry.

"So my whole life has been a complete sham?" He turned and glared at me now, as if I had planned this whole thing just to hurt him. "A total lie?"

"No, Jamie. It has not been a sham or a lie. You are who you are no matter who your parents were or what they did."

He narrowed his eyes and studied me. "So, are you *really* my mom?"

"Of course!"

"How do I know for sure? For all I know, you and Dad might've kidnapped me at birth. Maybe I have real parents living somewhere else right now. Maybe it's Barney and Martha Smith of Little Rock, Arkansas."

"It is *not* Barney and Martha Smith of Little Rock, Arkansas!"

"How do I know?"

"Why would I lie to you?"

He shook his head. "I don't know, Mom, you tell me. Why *did* you lie to me?"

"How in the world was I supposed to tell a little boy that his birth father had died? What difference did it make?"

"It makes a difference, Mom!"

"How? How could this change anything?"

"Remember all the crud I went through with Dad and not wanting to go into the shoe business?"

"Of course." I felt a small stab of guilt now. Perhaps I should have told him sooner.

"Well, maybe if I'd known that my real dad was actually someone else, well, maybe things would've made more sense."

"I don't see how."

"You said my *real* dad played piano too?"

I nodded without speaking.

"And something in me was just bursting to play piano, Mom. Don't you get that? And if I'd known, I could've told you and Dad the truth about quitting college and getting into music. It would've made sense."

I considered this. "And it would've hurt your dad, Jamie. He felt you were his son. He treated you like a son. He loved you, believed in you. We were his family. And when he married me, knowing full well that I was expecting, he only asked one thing."

"What?"

"For me to never mention a word about Liam again."

"You broke your promise, Mom."

"Not to Hal, I didn't. I never did say a word to him, or anyone, not while he was alive." I swallowed hard. "But I thought you had a right to know, Jamie. Would you rather I hadn't told you?"

He sat down and punched the pillow several times. "I don't know, Mom. I don't know much of anything at the moment. Except that you lied to me. My whole life has been nothing but a great big fabrication. James William Frederick is nothing but a fraud."

"That's not true, Jamie. You are blowing this way out of proportion."

"It's *my* life, Mom!" He stood and opened the door now, obviously a not-so-subtle hint that this conversation was over. "If I want to blow it out of proportion, or just blow altogether, well, I guess I can."

I stood and walked to the door. "Well, just know this, Jamie. Liam O'Neil was a fine man. A good man. And you are very much like him. And that's nothing to be ashamed of."

Jamie studied me. "Maybe I'm not ashamed of *him*, Mom."

I stared at my son. I knew what he was saying. He was ashamed of *me*. And why not? For all these years, I'd been ashamed of myself. It only made sense that he would feel the same.

12

Jamie

It felt like my world turned upside down this morning, or maybe inside out. But as soon as my mom left my hotel room, I packed a small bag and I took off. I wasn't sure where I was going or when I'd come back. All I knew was that I had to get away from her. It felt as if my mother had turned into someone else, like one of those weird B movies—a sci-fi or horror film—where aliens possess people, making them speak and act like complete strangers. That was what Mom seemed like to me. A complete stranger.

My parents raised me with a certain set of morals. Not that I'd always practiced them myself, obviously, but it was a standard I'd grown to accept and even respect—especially in my parents. It was comforting to know that they were rock solid and predictable. And I assumed that eventually I'd adhere to their standards myself.

But suddenly that whole thing seemed like a hoax, a great big charade where nothing was as it seemed. Everything about my life felt phony to me now. My dad had not been my *real* dad. The family business that he tried to force me into wasn't even my own family's business. My mother, the woman who always insisted on truth and integrity, had lived out a great big lie, a lie that was created to cover up her own indiscretions. It was like, while my back was turned, someone had dropped an H-bomb onto my life. In a split second, everything was changed.

I walked through town and just kept on going, following the road before me as I mulled over what had just happened, replaying all the words that had been said. After about an hour, I figured it was possible that I had overreacted to this. And yet, I felt like I'd been tricked or robbed or hoodwinked. And by my very own parents—rather, the people I had assumed were my parents. Now I knew that Dad, or Hal, really wasn't. Well, I supposed that explained some things about me. We were so completely different, he and I. And yet I really did like him. Oh, sure, I'd taken the poor guy for granted and I'd taken advantage of him. But after he died, I had realized how much I really did love him. I had decided that I even wanted to be like him—in time.

For some reason this whole thing reminded me of President Kennedy. His death had knocked me sideways too. I remembered how lost I'd felt after he was assassinated, so confused and hopeless and alone. And yet that was exactly how I felt again today—only more so. I grappled with the thought that I'd not only lost the man I'd called "Dad" for most of my life but now my biological father as well. A man I'd never even known—or known about. Well, it was just too much. It wasn't fair that all the father figures had been stripped from my life—*bam*—just like that.

I mulled over these things as I walked and walked, just following the curving country road to wherever it led and not thinking about whether or not I would follow it back again. After a couple of hours, I realized that I'd walked clear out of town and was now entering another town. Another sea town, but not as picturesque as Clifden, this one also had a large dock, and I noticed what appeared to be a ferryboat docked there. People who looked like they knew where they were going were starting to board, and I suddenly decided to see if I could join them.

I quickly located the small ticket office, and without having the slightest idea where Inishbofin might be, or even caring much, although it was the ferry's destination, I bought a roundtrip ticket and boarded the boat. Since the sun was still shining, although clouds were gathering on the western horizon, I sat out on the upper deck, waiting for the boat to sail, which it did rather quickly. Then, once it was moving away from the dock and cutting through the ocean, I felt a small wave of concern, or perhaps it was regret or remorse . . . I wasn't even sure. But I simply blocked these feelings away by focusing my eyes at the bright blue sea and the sky, wondering where I would ever fit into this mixed-up world. Maybe I should join the Navy instead of the Air Force.

After about twenty minutes, I actually started to get a little worried. The ferry appeared to be going straight out to sea, and suddenly I wondered just what I'd gotten myself into. Just where was Inishbofin anyway? I had assumed it was another small seaport on up the shore, but the mainland was quite a ways behind us now, and besides the big, blue sea and a bank of gray clouds, who knew what lie ahead? I wanted to ask another passenger for information, but realized how stupid that would make me sound. Why had this crazy American guy gotten onto a boat without even knowing where it was headed? Then, I reassured myself, these other passengers seemed perfectly normal and well adjusted. They appeared completely unconcerned over the fact that we seemed to be going due west, heading straight toward America. Obviously, they knew something I didn't, so why should I be worried?

Finally, I saw a mound of land up ahead, as well as something that looked like a fortress. Inishbofin had to be an island. Well, that was fine with me. I didn't mind exploring an Irish island to take my mind off of things.

"I've never been to Inishbofin," I said to a pretty girl who had just come out onto the deck. The wind was picking up now, and she was attempting to tie a pink scarf over her curly auburn hair. She looked to be about my age and had a nice sprinkling of freckles over an upturned nose. "Do you know much about the place?"

She laughed. "Probably a bit too much since I was born and raised there. Are you an American?"

"Yes." I smiled at her. "Just visiting."

"Seems an odd time to be visiting," she said. "What with holidays and all."

"Yes. Well, it was my mother's idea to spend Christmas in Ireland. We've been staying in Clifden."

She nodded. "I see. And ya decided to do some explorations on your own today?"

"That's right."

"Some say that Inishbofin is one of the loveliest islands in Ireland. And I suppose it does have some keen spots of interest, although I've taken them for granted myself, and I've known more than one tourist that got disappointed." She sighed, shading her eyes as she peered up ahead. "Still, I'm glad to be coming home for Christmas. I can't wait to see my family."

"Where have you been?" I asked.

"In Galway. I finished my nurses' training last year and I'm working for a pediatrician in the city now."

"So do you come home to visit a lot?"

"When I can. I suppose I do miss it a bit."

"Hello, Katie Flynn!" called an old man in a plaid jacket who had just made his way to the top deck. He was lighting up a pipe.

"Hello, Mr. Kelly." She waved, then turned back to me. "Inishbofin is a rather small place. Everyone knows everyone there."

"Then maybe I should introduce myself," I said. "My name is Jamie Frederick."

"And, as ya heard, my island friends call me Katie Flynn, although I go by Katherine in the city. It sounds a bit more sophisticated than Katie, don't ya think?"

"So, tell me, Katie, what do I do when I get to Inishbofin?"

She peered up at the sky. "Depending on the weather, which is about to change, there are a few things you could do."

"For instance."

"Well, on a good day there's plenty of fishing. And we do get scuba divers in the summertime. Of course, there's bird-watching, although it's not the best season for that right now, and we do have some gorgeous beaches . . ." She studied me for a moment. "Do ya know how to ride a bike, Jamie Frederick?"

I laughed. "Of course."

"Lots of tourists rent bikes. They tour the island that way. But you don't have to rent a bike. You come on by my house and I'll loan you one of my brothers' bikes."

I grinned at her. "But how will I find my way around the island?"

"It's a bit hard to get lost, ya know, we're not terribly big." Then she seemed to catch my clue. "I suppose I could show you about for a bit though. After I've spent some time with my family, that is—I can't be taking off as soon as I darken the door."

We continued to talk as the ferry pulled into the dock. Then Katie went below to get her bags, and we met again once we were on land. I carried my small bag as well as her larger suitcase, and we walked into town together. Then once we got to what appeared to be a main street, she paused and wrote some quick directions for getting to her house on a small slip of paper.

"Thanks," I told her, wondering what I'd do until she was freed up to take that little bike ride with me. It was already after two o'clock, and I didn't want to waste time.

"Looks to be gettin' thundery," she said, glancing up at the sky as she took her large suitcase from me.

"Thundery?"

"A storm's a-coming." She nodded to the big, rounded dark clouds that hovered directly overhead.

"Oh." I nodded. "Not so good for riding bikes then?"

She laughed. "Not unless you want to light up like a Christmas tree. You best keep inside. If I were you, I'd get myself checked into Murphy's straight away."

"Murphy's?"

"You do have a reservation, do you not?"

"For what?"

"For a room." She frowned at me.

"A room?"

She shook her head as if questioning my mental capacity. "For overnight, Jamie Frederick." Then she pointed back to the dock, which was empty now. The ferry was already making its way back to the mainland. "You do know that's the last ferry for the day, do you not?"

I felt my eyes getting wide. "The *last* ferry?"

"Aye." She glanced at my bag. "You did mean to stay the night, didn't ya?"

I took in a quick breath. "Oh, I hadn't really thought about it. But at least I came prepared." I forced a confident smile. "So, which way to Murphy's?"

She pointed to a large gray stone building with a sign that said MURPHY'S INN in bright blue letters. "That's it. I hope they have a room."

I wanted to ask if there was a room at her house, but thought better of it. I'd already shown her that I wasn't the smartest tourist around.

"Come by the house tomorrow," she called over her shoulder. "If the weather's willing, we can take a ride."

"Right." I waved good-bye and hurried over to Murphy's Inn. I just hoped it wouldn't turn out to be like Murphy's

Law and have no vacancy. I couldn't imagine sleeping out in the rain tonight.

After a brief explanation as to why I had no reservation, and an admission to my general American naïveté, I was eventually given a room.

"You're lucky we weren't full up," the woman said, "what with the holidays and all, we sometimes don't have a room to spare this time o' year."

"Is there a phone I can use?"

She looked at me as if I had two heads, then laughed. "A *telephone*?"

"Yes. I need to make a call."

"We do not trouble ourselves with such things."

"Are you telling me there are no phones in Inishbofin?"

She nodded, suppressing more laughter. "'Tis wha' I be telling you, laddie."

"Oh." I tried to regain a bit of composure as I picked up my key and my bag and made my way to my room, but I could hear her chuckling as she repeated my story to a man named Sean, who I supposed was her husband. Well, I told myself as I unlocked the door to a small and sparsely furnished room, maybe it was for the best not to call my mother just yet. Maybe she and I both still needed some time to stew, then cool down. Still, I felt a little guilty. And I knew she'd be worried.

My guilt was soon distracted by the "thundery" weather that quickly set in. The wind picked up and the thunder boomed. I left my bag in the room and decided to check out what I was guessing was the only pub in town, just a couple doors down from the inn. I'd just finished my first Guinness when the lights went out.

"Does this happen a lot?" I asked as the pub owner lit a kerosene lantern and a couple of candles as if this were no big deal.

"Now and again," he said as he blew out a match.

The wind was howling now. That, combined with the booms of thunder and flashes of lightning, and I wasn't too sure that I wanted to venture out on the streets just yet. What kind of a mess had I gotten myself into anyway?

"Do you serve food here?" I asked the pub owner. I was his only customer, and I had a feeling he wouldn't mind if I made myself scarce just now. But I also knew that although the Murphy Inn served breakfast, they didn't have an actual restaurant for the other meals. Plus I hadn't eaten anything since I'd put away a stale bag of pretzels and a lukewarm lemonade on the ferry today. My stomach was growling like a wild beast.

"I reckon the wife can fix somet'ing," he said, disappearing through a door that I figured must lead to some kind of living quarters. I was alone in the pub now, just me and the lantern and flickering candles. I longed for some music, but there was no jukebox or radio or anything to break the silence. Just the sound of the occasional clap of thunder, which usually made me jump.

After what seemed an unreasonable amount of time, and I was tempted to just leave, the pub owner came back with what appeared to be some sort of meat sandwich and a bowl of brown-looking soup. I ordered another pint to go with this and quickly ate. I couldn't say it was the best meal I'd ever had, but it certainly wasn't the worst either. I paid the man, setting on the counter what seemed like a generous tip for his wife.

"Thank ya," he said, as if he really did appreciate my business after all. "Mind the storm now, an' keep the wind to yer back."

I thanked him and pushed open the door just in time to get hit with a blast of wet wind. Fortunately, the inn was downwind, and propelled by the blustery air, I ran all the way. Even so, I was soaked by the time I got there. I paused in the tiny lobby to shake off some of the rain. It looked like the inn was without electricity too. Other than a smoky kerosene lantern on the registration desk, it was shadowy dark in here too.

"There ya are now." The woman who'd given me the room reached under the counter for something. "Ya haven't blown away with the storm then, have ya?" She handed me several white taper candles and a small box of matches. "Candleholders'll be in your room. This should get you through the night."

I thanked her, then headed up the stone stairs to my room. Fortunately someone had set out a couple of burning candles to light the way, but the shadows these cast on the old stone walls was a little eerie, and I felt I was starting to understand why the Irish had such a reputation for ghosts. The inn hadn't been exactly warm and cozy when I got here this afternoon, and I had a feeling it was going to feel pretty cold before the night was over. I lit a candle to see to unlock the door to my room, cautiously going inside. Before long I located several metal candleholders in the drawer of a small dresser over by the window. I lit two of the candles and set them out, then peeled off my soggy fisherman knit sweater and hung it over a wooden chair, hoping that it would dry, or at least be slightly less damp, by morning.

It wasn't even seven o'clock now, but I knew there was nothing to do in this place. I wasn't the least bit sleepy, and after several minutes of shivering in the cold and dimly lit room, I got into bed just hoping to get warmed up a bit. I kicked my feet back and forth in an attempt to defrost the sheets, but it seemed useless. Why had I come here anyway? What had I been thinking? Obviously, I wasn't thinking at all. Otherwise I'd be back at the relatively nice hotel with heat and electricity—maybe off listening to music in one of the local pubs and eating something that actually tasted good.

What a fool I'd been to go stomping off like that. Oh, sure, it had been hard and shocking to hear what Mom told me—it still was. But why had I reacted so strongly? What good had it done? And what was I thinking to hop on a boat without knowing where it was headed? Look where it had gotten me—locked up in this dark dungeonlike room on a tiny island where the next ferry to the mainland wouldn't be until tomorrow. What a complete imbecile I'd been! You'd think a "grown" man of twenty-one would have more sense.

Then I began to wonder about the man who had been my biological father. I wondered how old he might have been when he and my mom had met. Perhaps he'd been about my age. Maybe he'd faced the same kinds of questions I struggled with now. I wondered what he looked like and how he felt about going to war or what it felt like to be in Pearl Harbor when it was attacked that day. *Liam O'Neil.* Who had that guy really been? A musician who'd graduated from Annapolis? And hadn't Mom said he'd been an officer in the Navy? But how long had he been in the Navy? And what about his family, who would also be my family? Did I have aunts, uncles, cousins? And what about the fact that his parents had come from Ireland? Were any of their relatives still here now?

Maybe that's why I felt such an affinity for this country—the Emerald Isle. Well, until today, that is. I wasn't too sure how I felt about Ireland, particularly Inishbofin, at the moment. Mostly it felt inhospitable. It was cold and damp and dark, and I wanted to get out of this place, the sooner the better. But Ireland, in general, meaning the people, the music, the land . . . it had all seemed to speak to me at first, to welcome me, as if I actually belonged. And then when I'd finally sat down at a piano—was that only just yesterday?—it had all seemed to fall right into place for me. I had begun to feel as if I was finding myself, knowing who I was and what I wanted out of life. But then came my mother's stunning confession, and now, stuck in this strange and isolated island called Inishbofin, I'd never felt so lost in my life. Lost and alone and hopeless.

Still shivering, I wondered if it was only because of my birth father that Mom had brought me to Ireland. There really seemed no other logical explanation. And, really, it made some sense. I could imagine her planning this whole thing, assuming it would be the perfect way to break the news to me—Mom had always cared a lot about settings and doing things in certain ways. And I had to give her credit, coming probably had been a good idea, but then I'd gone and messed it all up. I felt pretty certain that I'd derailed my mother when I confessed about college and squandering my tuition money. I'm sure I threw a great big wrench in her works.

Maybe it had something to do with freezing to death and being stuck somewhere I'd rather not be—a prison of sorts—but I felt that the time had come to get honest with myself. And I had to admit I'd probably overreacted to Mom's revelation in order to create a smoke screen of sorts. It was my sorry little attempt to cover my own mistakes. I'd blown her revelation out of proportion just to get the limelight off of me and back onto her.

Sometimes the truth was ugly.

Still, and to be fair, I was pretty stunned to think that Mom—*my mom*—had been involved *like that* with another man. And they weren't even married. It was equally shocking to think that she'd then married my dad, rather Hal, while pregnant with another man's child. Man, she would've had a fit if I'd pulled a stunt like that. My mom, the same woman who'd given me all those speeches about what kind of girls were nice and what kind were not, back when I first started dating. But didn't this change things? How could my mom have been so opinionated about what she called "fast" girls. Was it possible that she had been a "fast" girl herself? I even recalled how sometimes, like right before a date, she pressured my dad into giving me *the speech*, although it made him extremely uncomfortable, even more so than for her. Now I had an idea of why she'd been so worried that I might get a girl "in trouble." She'd been a girl "in trouble" once. It was really mind-blowing.

I'd heard the phrase "dark night of the soul" before, I think it was in my English lit class, but I guess that would pretty much describe how I felt that night in Inishbofin. Combine thunder, lightning, darkness, and lack of heat with an overall lost feeling, and I couldn't recall a darker or longer night. And before the torturous night was to end, and before I would finally find relief in sleep, I wrestled with many demons. I had moments when I questioned the state of my mind—I wondered if maybe this was all my own doing. Then finally I remembered how Dad, the dad who raised me, had always told me that *God was there in times of trouble.*

"God wants you to call out to him, Jamie." Dad told me this right before I set off on that crazy summer road trip—the last time I'd seen him alive. "God knows you're going to have some hard times and challenges ahead, son, and that's okay. He just wants you to know that he's there, always ready to help. He's a lifeline. Just grab onto him and don't let go."

At the time I'd taken those words completely in stride. To be polite, I had even pretended to listen, but I knew I'd dismiss his advice, right along with most of the other parental warnings that were so generously dished out whenever I got ready to attempt something new. And that's exactly what I did. I felt that I had control of things, that I was the master of my own fate, and that I could do whatever I pleased and everything would turn out just fine.

But suddenly I wasn't so sure about that. In fact, I wasn't so sure about much of anything. Maybe the time had really come to call out to God. Maybe I wasn't doing such a fantastic job of handling everything on my own. And so, after struggling with my demons and my selfishness and the cold and the dark of the night, I finally did cry out to God. I did admit my weaknesses, my failings, my insecurities, and my fears. And then I cried like a baby, crying to God. And I pleaded with him to help me. And at last I went to sleep.

13

Colleen

I felt like a cat on a hot tin roof as I got ready for bed. Not that it was particularly warm in Ireland, especially since a storm had stirred up that evening. But I felt edgy and anxious and unable to settle down. As far as I knew, Jamie had not returned to the hotel at any time today. At least no one had seen him. For a while I'd held out the faint hope that perhaps he'd sneaked in when the clerk was away from the desk, but I'd tried knocking on Jamie's door just a few minutes ago and there was no answer. Still, I reminded myself, it wouldn't be the first night my son had stayed out late. And I had no doubts that he needed some time to himself just now. For that matter, so did I.

Now, I hadn't expected this to be easy. But I'd hoped it would go more smoothly than it had. I had known my news would be a shock to Jamie, but I had no idea it would drive such a wedge between us. Perhaps it had been unrealistic to think that Jamie would be interested in hearing about his biological father. Yet somehow I had convinced myself that once he recovered from the shock, he would've been understanding, perhaps even compassionate. And I'd thought he'd have questions. But, as I'd walked the streets of Clifden earlier today, I'd come to grips with the possibility that I'd been wrong. Perhaps about everything.

The next morning, after I'd had breakfast and waited what seemed a reasonable amount of time for a young man to sleep in after a late night, I tried knocking on Jamie's door again. Still no answer. It was nearly ten o'clock and I'd kept a close eye on the front door while eating, so I felt certain he hadn't slipped past me and gone out again. I knocked even louder now, calling out his name. But the door remained firmly shut. Silent. That's when I suspected that he hadn't returned to the hotel at all last night. But, if that was the case, where could he be? He didn't have too much money on him. Oh, enough for a night or two in another hotel and some meals. But he didn't have enough to get far away, and if he did, he wouldn't last long.

The storm that had started up yesterday evening grew even more violent as the following day wore on. By midmorning, the wooden shutters on the ocean side of the hotel had been closed up tight, blocking the light and giving the interior of my room a dark and somber appearance. Despite the dismal-looking weather, I took a morning walk, which was really an excuse to search for my son again, but I noticed shopkeepers taking signs and things inside, and they too were closing shutters, bolting things down tight.

"The cat's tail is in the hot ashes," an old woman said as she scurried away from the grocery store with a bag of provisions. I had no idea what she meant by this strange comment, but her eyes looked foreboding. Also, the wind whipped at my skirt, slapping it back and forth against my legs as I walked back to the hotel. It seemed that everyone in town was holing up and hiding out, and as I rushed into the lobby, followed by a gust, I was informed by the hotel manager that we might be in for "a class ten gale."

"What does that mean?" I asked.

"It means ya best stay inside unless ya want to be blown clear to Dublin." Then he hurried off, I felt sure, to batten down more hatches.

As far as I could tell, Jamie still wasn't back yet. He didn't answer his door, and when I pressed my ear to it, all I heard was silence—that and the howling of the wind outside. Now I was beginning to feel seriously alarmed. What if he was out in the elements during this storm? Maybe he wasn't aware that we were in for a class ten gale, whatever that might be. Or what if he'd been hurt or was in some kind of danger? Once again, anything and everything seemed possible.

Suddenly I felt completely enraged by my wayward son. That he dared to do this to me—*his mother*—that he dared to treat me like this! After all I'd done for him, all I'd given up to secure his future, making sure that he had everything he needed, everything he wanted, setting my own needs and feelings aside! After all that—that he would put me through something like this—it seemed unpardonable. All I'd ever done in my life, every decision I'd ever made, every sacrifice . . . it had all been for Jamie. Well, for Jamie and Hal. But everything about my whole life had been to make them happy. It had always been my primary focus and concern. And this was the thanks I got?

I probably spent a couple of hours going through this rage, working my way through these feelings, trying to make sense of what seemed totally senseless.

I finally wore myself down. No more rage, no more fury. These emotions were replaced with worry. And so, as I sat alone in my darkened room with shuttered windows just waiting for this storm to pass, my imagination was assaulted with all the horrible possibilities. Instead of being angry at Jamie, I became obsessed over his safety. Where could he be during this horrible storm? What if he was injured? Or dead? Finally I knew that my only recourse was to pray. It was all I had left. But, as I prayed, I couldn't help but imagine how my life might be without my son. And that picture was bleak and dismal.

I'd never wanted to be one of those controlling mothers, the kind of women who doted on an only child, expecting that son or daughter to bring fulfillment and happiness to her, a comfort in her old age, make a life where none existed. I didn't really want that and I knew that wasn't fair. It was selfish and wrong. And yet I just didn't think I could survive losing Jamie. I'd lost Liam twenty-two years ago, and not long after that I'd lost my father, and then most recently Hal. How much more loss could I handle?

"I can't take any more!" I yelled out to God. The wind was blowing so loudly now that I wasn't even concerned that other guests would hear me. "I don't think I can stand it!" I cried. Then, pouring out all my tumultuous feelings and heartaches and worries, it was as if I just dumped the whole sorry load at God's feet. Finally, I had nothing more to say, nothing more to do, nothing more to think. I felt completely emptied. And yet somehow I believed that God could deal with it.

For the first time in my life, I knew I must completely trust God to handle this. Or maybe I was simply at the end of my rope with no place left to turn. Perhaps for the first time ever, I realized that there was really nothing I could do to control anything. Not a single thing. Just one look at my life, and it should've been obvious to me long ago. For, no matter how hard I tried to hold it together, whether it had been with Liam or Hal or Jamie . . . it had never worked. Or if it appeared to work, it was only a temporary illusion. A false moment. Because then, just as if a class ten gale had swept through, it could all be blown away. Just like that—now you see it, now you don't. It was gone. I might as well give it up.

Somehow I fell into an exhausted sleep in the midst of the storm, and when I woke up, everything was quiet. The weather outside and my internal storm had both quit howling. I left my room and knocked on Jamie's door, but still no answer. And yet I didn't feel terribly upset by this. It was as if something in me had simply let go, and I knew it was up to God to work this thing out. I returned to my room, got on my coat, and went downstairs to inquire about my son. Just in case.

"I haven't seen him," the desk clerk said. "But if da lad was smart, he'd a stayed put during that storm. 'Twas a bad one."

"Is it over now?"

He nodded. "Aye. It seems to be. Go outside and have a look for yourself."

So I went outside and was surprised to see that not only had the sky cleared up, but the sun, now dipping low into the western horizon, was shining its spotlight onto a wet and sparkling world, and there was a glorious rainbow out over the ocean. And the crisp sea air was so fresh I wanted to drink it! But the day was coming to a swift end, and although it was barely four o'clock, it would soon be dark again. And yet I still didn't feel that sense of panic that I'd felt earlier. Something in me, probably my strong will, had completely surrendered itself to God during today's storm. For the first time in my life, I felt that I was really in his hands. Even with Jamie missing in a foreign country, I felt at peace. And I *would* get through this. God would help me.

I ate a quiet and early dinner at the hotel, and although I still found myself thinking of Jamie, it wasn't that old obsessive sort of fearful thinking. I wrapped my thoughts of my son in layers of prayers. And I eventually was able to go up to my room and to bed—and finally to sleep.

The following morning, I wasn't quite sure what to do. This was the third day that I had not seen my son, and despite my resolve to trust God, it was becoming more of a challenge. After all, I did have a missing son. I considered calling the authorities, but I had no idea what I'd say—and would I need to tell them that we'd had a squabble? And, if so, would they even take me seriously? I thought about asking the manager for advice, but wasn't really sure that it would do much good. Finally I thought about Kerry and the Anchor Inn. She seemed such a wise and caring soul and the only actual friend I had in Connemara. And so, since the weather had continued to be clear today, I decided to walk on up there in time for afternoon tea. I was surprised to see some trees had fallen and some roofs had lost shingles and tiles and a small boat had blown onto shore. But other than that, it was a splendid day with sunshine and temperatures much warmer than the previous week. And as I walked up the hill toward the Anchor Inn, I was stunned by the gorgeous view of sea and sky. Really breathtaking!

As I walked up to the restaurant, I hoped that I hadn't made a mistake in coming up here. I didn't see any cars or signs of customers. Perhaps they weren't even open.

"Welcome, welcome," Kerry called out as she opened the door for me, waving me inside. "Isn't it a lovely day!"

I smiled at her. "Yes. A perfect afternoon for tea."

Soon we were seated at a small table near the fireplace, and I was pouring out my story, or most of it. And, once again, she proved a sympathetic listener.

"So you haven't seen the lad in three days?" she said as Dolan set a rose-covered porcelain teapot on our table, along with a silver plate of cookies and miniature tea sandwiches, all prettily arranged on a paper doily.

I shook my head. "And I'm not sure what to do about it."

"But ya did tell him about his father, the way you'd planned to?"

I nodded now. "Unfortunately, that seemed to be the final straw." Out of respect for Jamie, I hadn't told her about his surprising confession that came first.

She frowned. "Jamie seemed a sensible lad, to me. Perhaps he only needed a bit of time—to clear his head so to speak."

"I thought about that too. But now that he's been gone two nights . . ." I sighed. "Well, I'm just not sure. What if something happened to him?"

She waved her hand as if to dismiss my concerns. "Oh, now, what could've happened? Jamie is a strapping young man and I'm sure he's quite able to look out for himself. Don't ya think?"

"Yes, I hope so . . ."

"But you're a bit worried all the same."

"I'm really trying to trust God right now." I paused, wondering how much I wanted to share about this—in some ways it seemed rather personal, and yet . . . "You see, I've been such a worrier, and I spent so much time and energy trying to control everything about my life . . . and only recently I came to understand that, well, it seems I really can't control much of anything."

"Isn't that the truth?"

"So I might as well trust God."

"Sometimes 'tis all we can do." She refilled both of our dainty teacups. "'Tis a long road that has no turning, Colleen."

"What does that mean?"

She seemed to consider this. "It means it may take him awhile to get there, my friend, but your Jamie will eventually find his way home—meaning home to you."

"I hope you're right."

"What are you two doing for Christmas Day?" she asked, and I suspected she had changed the subject for my benefit.

"Goodness," I said, trying to remember what day it was today. "I'd almost forgotten all about Christmas."

"'Tis only a few days off now."

"I hadn't really thought that far ahead," I admitted. "To be honest, what with how things have gone lately, if Jamie were to come back today, I'd just as soon change my flight and go back home immediately and we'd have Christmas at home."

She frowned. "So you've gone sour on our country already?"

I thought about this. "No, I really *do* love Ireland. But what with the storm yesterday . . . and Jamie being gone . . . well, I suppose I feel that it might be safer to be at home for the holidays." Then I laughed. "Oh, there I go, thinking I can control things again."

"If you and Jamie find yourselves still here in Ireland by next week, I hope you'll come on up to the old Anchor for Christmas dinner. We stay open for some of the older folks in town, ones who have no family about, and I'd be pleased to have you join us. We'll have turkey and goose and all of the trimmings. Dinner is at two."

"Thank you, Kerry. That sounds wonderful, and I'll keep that in mind."

"And tell your wayward laddie, *when* he comes home, that I'd be delighted to hear him play again. In fact, we have quite a crowd coming tonight. Dolan said we are almost full up. But then it's the Saturday before Christmas, and folks like to go out, so it's not so unusual."

I frowned. "Well, I don't even know that Jamie will be back today."

She patted my hand. "Aye, I understand. Whether he comes back tonight or next week, just know that you're both welcome . . . anytime."

The clear weather had continued to hold out, and so I walked back to town, praying as I went. Then, just as I turned the corner to the hotel, I noticed a familiar figure walking down the street directly toward me.

"Jamie!" I cried, as I ran toward him, throwing my arms out to embrace him. "I'm so happy to see you!"

"I'm really sorry, Mom," he said immediately. "I know you must've been worried and I couldn't—"

"Never mind about that," I said, which I knew must sound crazy after I made such a big deal of this only days ago. "I'm just relieved that you're safe and sound."

"I really would've called you, Mom." He kept one arm wrapped protectively around my shoulders as we walked side by side toward the hotel. "But I went to this island and then the storm hit and there were no phones and—"

"What?" I blinked at him as he held open the door to the hotel. "No phones?" Hopefully my son hadn't taken up the gift of blarney while he'd been gone. Come to think of it, maybe he'd been born with it.

"Yeah, Mom," he continued as we went into the lobby. "This place is called Inishbofin and they really don't have phones there and—"

"Ah, so that's where ya been, laddie," said the desk clerk, the one I'd haunted with my regular inquiries regarding the possible whereabouts of my long-lost son. "'Tis no wonder you were not able to make it back, nor to call your ma."

"Why's that?" I asked him.

"The ferryboat captain will not go out to the island during a class ten gale." He looked at me as if questioning my state of mind for not already knowing this. "And, certainly, Inishbofin has no telephones. Everyone knows that."

I turned and stared at my son in disbelief. "You were really there? Out on this island with no phones?"

He laughed. "Yeah, trust me, Mom, this isn't the kind of thing a guy makes up."

14

Jamie

Mom and I got a cup of coffee in the hotel restaurant, and I told her all about my strange visit in Inishbofin, which I learned was Irish for *Island of the White Cow*, and I actually thought might make a good name for a band if I ever started one again. Probably better than Jamie and the Muskrats. Apparently that name was the result of someone a few centuries back seeing a white cow there during a dense fog. I asked my new friend Katie how anyone could see a white cow through dense fog, and she just laughed.

"I got stuck on the island for two long nights," I explained, "all because of that storm and the ferryboat not coming. And it was pretty creepy for a while. But by yesterday afternoon, the storm cleared up and Katie gave me a bicycling tour of the island, which was actually kind of interesting. Then this morning, before the ferry came, she took me to see these amazing tide pools."

"Really?" Mom looked impressed.

"Yeah, at first all I wanted to do was to get out of that place. I mean, it felt like a prison and, man, was it ever cold and wet. And, oh yeah, did I mention that they lost their electricity?"

"Sounds like quite an experience."

"You got that right. But now I'm glad I went and I'd like to go back again, maybe just for a day. Only I'd make sure to tell you. I really did feel bad about being AWOL and not able to call—especially after I got stuck there for the second day. I knew you'd be frantic."

Then Mom told me about how it was actually good for her having me gone, and how she really learned to pray and to trust God. "I need to lean on God more," she admitted. "Instead of trying to hold everything together myself."

"Yeah," I told her. "I kind of learned the same thing too."

"I know it's just the beginning for me," she said, "and I have a feeling there are still a lot of things I need to work out . . ."

"Like what?" I was starting to see Mom with a new set of eyes. She wasn't just Mom anymore. She had been in love with a man I'd never known, kept this hidden for years. It really was pretty mysterious.

She studied me, as if trying to decide how much to say. Then she sighed. "Things about your dad . . ."

"You mean Hal, that dad?"

She smiled faintly. "Yes, that dad. Sometimes I feel that I cheated him, Jamie. I feel guilty that I didn't love him enough."

"Oh, Mom." I reached over and put my hand over hers. "Like I told you before, Dad was 'over the moon' for you.

I don't know how you could've possibly made him any happier."

She shook her head. "But I feel guilty."

"Look," I began, "you told Dad what was up before you guys got married, right?"

"Of course."

"He knew exactly what he was getting into."

She nodded.

"And he was thrilled about it. You were a really good wife to him. You made him happy. And I know he was proud of you. He loved everything about you, the way you took care of us, your cooking, your housekeeping, your looks—the works. Honestly, Mom, what more could you have done?"

She sighed. "I don't know . . ."

"You gotta let that go."

Now she smiled at me. "You're probably right."

"I know I'm right."

Mom laughed. "Oh, the confidence of youth."

"You should've seen me the night of the storm," I admitted. "I didn't look too confident then."

"I almost forgot," Mom said. "I went to see Kerry at the Anchor Inn today, and she invited us to join them at the restaurant for Christmas Day."

I slapped my forehead. "Man, I almost forgot Christmas. When is it anyway?"

"Wednesday."

I nodded, reminding myself to pick up a present for her. It seemed the least I could do, considering how I must've worried her. And I was impressed with how she was taking everything so well. It seemed like we'd really moved on now.

"And Kerry invited you to come up and play the piano again."

"Really? That'd be cool." But suddenly I wasn't so sure. What if it was hard on Mom hearing me play? What if it reminded her too much of my father? "But, you know, I don't have to . . ."

"But don't you want to?"

"Of course, I *want* to. But not if you don't want me to. I remember how it was that night, the first time you heard me play . . ."

"Oh, I loved hearing you play, Jamie. It was just, well, you know . . . everything I told you. About Liam and all. That was hard. But I do love hearing you play."

"Maybe we could go up there tonight," I said, glancing at the clock. "It's getting close to dinnertime anyway."

Mom frowned slightly now.

"That's okay . . ." I had a feeling that she didn't really want to go, and although I wanted to understand this, it made me feel bad too.

"I know what you're thinking," she said quickly. "But you're wrong. I really do love hearing you play. In fact, I've decided to get a piano when we get back home."

"You mean if the house hasn't been sold," I teased.

"Even if it does sell. I'd still get a piano for the next house."

I considered telling her about my old secondhand piano, but figured that could wait. "But you don't want to go to the Anchor Inn tonight?"

"I think I'm a little worn out. I already walked up there and back once today. And I just had a lovely tea with Kerry." She paused. "Why don't you go on up there and play tonight, if you like. Then, if you aren't tired of the place, we could go up there again tomorrow. You could ask Kerry to reserve a table for us on Sunday night."

"Really, you don't mind?"

"Not at all." She smiled brightly. "I'm just so glad that you're back. And that we're okay. I think it'd be wonderful if you went up there. And I know Kerry will be so happy to see you."

"Cool!" I studied Mom closely. "I'm really interested in hearing more about Liam. And I'm curious about where his parents were from. Do you think I might have any living relatives in Ireland?"

She nodded. "I think it's a possibility. And all I can remember was that Liam wanted to come to Connemara someday. It was the first time I'd heard of the place, but it stuck in my mind."

"Wow, so he could have relatives around here?"

"Maybe so. Although I know a lot of people emigrated about the same time as his parents did. I'd meant to ask around, about the name O'Neil, but I haven't really gotten around to it yet. I guess I was a little distracted . . ."

"Sorry. Maybe we can both check around some. Did you ask Kerry if she knew any O'Neils?"

She shook her head. "I told her about Liam and all that, but I don't think I even mentioned his last name . . . we were talking about so many things."

"We'll have to see what we can find out," I said.

We talked awhile longer, but I think Mom could tell I was getting antsy, and she finally suggested I head on up there.

"Are you sure?" I asked, feeling a little guilty for leaving her.

She winked at me. "Yes, I'm absolutely positive. I'm actually looking forward to a quiet evening with my book."

I knew she meant an evening when she didn't have to be worried about her mixed-up son, but I didn't say this. "Well, I better go change." I nodded down to my fisherman knit sweater. "I finally got this thing dried out, but I'm sure it doesn't smell too fresh after all the weather and everything I've been through."

She laughed. "Maybe we can find a dry cleaners."

So I freshened up, and although it was dark, I went ahead and walked on up to the restaurant. Kerry was so warm when she welcomed me that I felt right at home. The place wasn't full, but lots busier than last time, and Dolan insisted on bringing me some complimentary fish and chips even before I sat down to play.

"Don't ya even think of paying," he whispered as he set the plate down, "or my sister will be fit to be tied."

I hurried to finish my dinner, went to wash my hands, then sat down to play. It felt so good to have my hands on the keys again. It was as if they belonged there. And, even though I hadn't played for several days, it seemed that my playing had actually improved. Or else it just felt like it. The diners clapped their approval after each piece, and when I took a little break to have a sip of the lemon soda that Donal had brought me, Kerry approached the piano with an attractive blonde woman with her. I was guessing that the woman was about my mom's age.

"This is my dear friend," Kerry said. "She was so impressed with your playing that she wanted to meet you. Margaret, I'd like to introduce you to my young American friend, Jamie Frederick."

The woman stared at me with a curious expression. "You play quite well, Jamie Frederick." Her accent was Irish, but something about her appearance seemed American. Maybe it was her pink knit dress. It reminded me of something my mother might wear.

"Thank you."

"It's a most unusual style," she said, glancing over her shoulder as if she were nervous about something. "*Very* unusual, I'd say."

I shrugged. "Well, I'm sort of self-taught. I kind of do my own thing."

"Interesting . . . you taught yourself to play piano?"

"That's right." I studied her, curious as to why she didn't go back to her table so I could continue to play.

"And you're an American?"

I nodded. Kerry had returned to the kitchen by now, and I wasn't quite sure what more I could say to this lady, but I figured I should be friendly, even if her questioning did make me uneasy. Who was she anyway? "Yeah, I used to play guitar and I had my own band"—I rambled just to fill the space—"but then I got interested in piano and just took it up on my own. I took a few music classes, but haven't had any real piano lessons or anything."

Her pale eyebrows lifted slightly. "That's quite impressive."

"Thanks." I smiled at her, wondering if perhaps she was some kind of music professor or a recording person. Who knew? At least she seemed to like my music. Still, I wished she'd leave. Something about those pale blue eyes just staring at me as if I were a monkey in the zoo made my skin sort of crawl.

"The way you play . . . your style . . . it reminds me of someone." Again, she glanced over her shoulder, then back at me with an odd expression. I was starting to feel like a character in *The Twilight Zone*. *The* Irish *Twilight Zone*.

"Yeah?" What was this lady after anyway? Was she a groupie? Did she think I was famous and wanted an autograph?

"Yes. You play in a style very similar to my good friend . . . and what's even odder is that you look quite a bit like him—or rather the way he looked when he was about your age. You could almost be brothers."

I suddenly remembered what my mom had said about my biological father and how I played piano and looked so much like him. Could she possibly know a relative of mine? Or maybe she'd known him, long ago. I felt my heart starting to pound now, like something really weird was going on here, but I couldn't think of a thing to say.

"Would you mind if I introduced him to you?"

"Who?" I managed to blurt out.

She waved to a table in the corner of the room. "My friend William," she said.

"Oh . . ." I took in a quick breath, trying to steady myself although I was still seated. "Sure."

She waved to a middle-aged man now, motioning him over here. He slowly stood and, using a cane, walked toward the piano with a slight limp. He was a nice-looking guy, fairly tall, with dark hair.

"William," Margaret said, "this is Jamie Frederick. I was just complimenting him on his fine musical abilities."

I stood and the man shook my hand. Now I could see his hair was tinged with gray at the temples, and he peered at me with a pair of intensely blue eyes—eyes that seemed familiar somehow.

"I'm so pleased to meet you, Jamie. I was taken aback by your distinctive style of music. Perhaps Margaret mentioned it, but I play in a similar style and I have to say it's not something you hear every day." His accent was mostly Irish, but I sensed a hint of an American mixed in there as well.

"Jamie just told me that he's self-taught," Margaret said.

William seemed to consider this. "That's how I learned too."

My heart had started to pound again. It thumped against my chest, reminding me of when I'd played the bass drum in marching band. Something really strange seemed to be going on here. I couldn't explain it, but I felt as if I already knew this man. "Excuse me," I said without allowing myself time to reconsider. "But do you know anyone by the name of O'Neil?"

Margaret blinked. "William's last name is O'Neil."

I sank down to the padded piano bench now, unsure as to whether I really heard her correctly or if I was imagining this. "Your name is William O'Neil?" I said slowly, letting it sink it. William, not Liam.

He nodded. "Yes, that's right."

"By any chance, did you have a brother by the name of *Liam*?"

Margaret laughed. "Liam is a nickname for William." She nodded to William. "He used to go by Liam when he was younger. Didn't you, William?"

He nodded, but his eyes were fixed tightly on me.

I reached for my glass and took a big gulp of soda. The bubbles burned as it went down, making my eyes water.

"Are you feeling all right, Jamie?" Margaret asked. "You don't look well."

By now Kerry had returned. "How are you doing, Jamie? Dolan said some of the folks are asking if you're going to play again. They so enjoy your music."

"He seems unwell," Margaret said.

I looked up at Kerry and swallowed hard. "Margaret just told me that Liam is a nickname for William."

Kerry looked puzzled by my curious statement, but she just chuckled and picked up my soda glass and sniffed at it. "Is that all you've been drinking tonight, laddie?"

I nodded uneasily, but continued anyway. I needed to know the truth, the sooner the better. "You see, my father's name was *Liam O'Neil.*"

Now they all looked slightly shocked, and I felt pretty stunned myself. I couldn't believe I'd just said this out loud. Good grief, there must've been hundreds of William O'Neils in Ireland. And, yet, I knew. Something in me just knew.

"What is your mother's name?" William asked in a quiet voice.

"Colleen."

William took in a deep breath, clasping his hand to his chest as if in pain. *"Colleen Johnson?"*

"Johnson was my mother's maiden name."

"May I sit down?" he asked slowly, steadying himself with one hand on the piano, the other clinging to his polished wooden cane.

I scooted over and made room for him on the bench beside me.

"Are you okay, William?" Margaret asked, her voice filled with concern.

He was taking slow deep breaths, and for a moment I thought perhaps he was having a heart attack. Just like my other father. Maybe I was a jinx—older men should keep their distance from me. Then William turned and looked at me with kind eyes. "How old are you, Jamie?"

"I'm twenty-one, sir. I was born July 27, 1942."

William took in another slow breath and just stared at me as if I were an apparition, then he slowly nodded again, as if this was all beginning to make perfect sense. His voice was calm now, but his hands trembled as he wrapped them around his cane. "I tried and tried to locate your dear mother . . ." He closed his eyes for a moment, as if trying to remember something long ago. "Johnson was such a common name . . . I called every Johnson in the Los Angeles area, asking for a Colleen May Johnson. I tried to find her old roommate. But it was as if they had both disappeared. I wondered if I'd imagined Colleen Johnson. But I knew she was real. I did an exhausting search for her, but with no luck. After a year or so, I even wondered if she had died."

"She thought you'd been killed in Pearl Harbor," I told him.

He sighed. "Nearly . . ." He put his hand on my shoulder and I could see tears in his eyes. "Your mother was the only thing that kept me alive. I wanted to get back to her."

"Come, come," Kerry said, taking me by the arm. "You both go on over to that quiet table over there and sit down. You need to talk about these things in private."

Soon we were seated by ourselves, and we both just sat and stared at each other for several long moments. It was so much to take in, and I think we were both in shock. Dolan had set a whiskey in front of William and a glass of water in front of me.

"I can't believe it," he finally said.

I shook my head. "Me neither."

He asked me questions and I told him what I knew. How my mother thought he had died, how she had married my dad. "Well, I guess he wasn't really my dad," I explained. "But I thought he was. Just until recently . . . my mom only told me the truth a few days ago."

"This is so amazing . . . so incredible . . ." He shook his head again. "I can just hardly believe it." He reached across the table and grasped my forearm, giving it a squeeze. "You're really here? You're really my son? It's like a dream."

I nodded. "Yeah, I feel the same. So what happened? Mom said you were an officer in the Navy, that you'd gone to Honolulu, but that you weren't supposed to be there long."

"I had gone to work on some communications things . . . on the SS *Arizona*. I'd only been there a couple of days when we were attacked. So many people died that day. I should've been one of them." He nodded toward his lap. "I lost my left leg in the explosion, lost so much blood that it was a wonder I survived at all. I don't actually remember much of it because I had a severe blow to the head and a concussion. The story I heard was that someone picked me out of the water, put a tourniquet on, and got me to a hospital. I was out of it for weeks, and when I came to, I kept thinking of Colleen. I would imagine her face, and that kept me alive."

"Wow."

"You can say that again. It really was a miracle."

"And Mom didn't know you were alive?"

"I sent letters to her address, but they were returned."

"The same happened to her."

"That may be because I wasn't considered officially stationed in Honolulu at the time. I'd only gone over to do some work, after that I was supposed to return to San Diego for further orders. And it's possible that I was listed as missing in action for a while. The world was a mess back then."

"And then Mom got married," I said sadly. "And her name changed. No wonder you couldn't find her."

I asked him more questions and discovered that he'd been living in Ireland since the late forties. "After the war and all . . . I just couldn't find anywhere I felt at home in America again," he said. "I drifted from town to town, job to job, and finally I came over here to visit and liked it so well that I never went back to America."

"I like it here too."

Then he asked me lots and lots of questions. I told him my whole life story, and he sat there and listened to me as if

I were the most exciting guy in the world. Ironic, considering all that he'd been through.

"I hate to ruin the party," Kerry said, "but we've been closed for nearly an hour."

I glanced at my watch. "Man, it's nearly eleven."

So William and Margaret and the couple with them gave me a ride back to town. "Is it all right if I call you tomorrow?" he asked as they dropped me in front of the hotel.

"Sure," I told him, getting out. "My mom is going to have a fit."

"A fit?" Margaret said.

"American slang," William said, winking at me.

Then I got out and waved, but as I went into the hotel, I had to wonder . . . what would Mom think of this? I'd have to be careful how I broke it to her—she might have a heart attack for real!

15

Colleen

It wasn't even seven in the morning when I heard knocking at my door. I sleepily pulled on my robe, then opened it to find Jamie standing in the hallway. He had an odd expression—I couldn't quite read it.

"Is something wrong?" I asked instinctively, then noticing that he was fully dressed, added, "Have you been out *all* night?"

"No and no," he said quickly. "I just got up really early and I couldn't wait for you to sleep any longer."

I smiled as I fastened the belt of my robe. "Now, isn't that a switch."

"Can you get dressed and come to breakfast?"

"Can I have twenty minutes?"

He frowned with impatience. "Yeah, I guess."

"Be right down." I closed the door and hurried to clean up and quickly dress, barely putting on makeup or doing my hair. I could tell by his nervous demeanor that despite his claim that nothing was wrong, something most definitely was up. I hoped it wasn't anything serious. Had he gotten into some sort of trouble when he'd been on that island, Inabobbin or whatever it was called? As I pushed my feet into my shoes, I reminded myself that worrying would not help. I remembered my resolve to trust God. And so as I hurried downstairs, I prayed. *Please, let me take whatever this is calmly. Let me trust you implicitly, God, and help me to remember that you are able to fix anything. Amen.*

"You're here," Jamie said brightly, pulling out a chair for me. We were the only ones in the restaurant and I wasn't even sure they were open yet, although I thought I smelled coffee drifting from the kitchen area.

"What is going on?" I asked in a controlled voice, forcing a smile. "You have me quite curious."

He slowly inhaled, then placed both of his hands palms down on the table and exhaled. "You are *not* going to believe this, Mom."

I thought I could feel my blood pressure rise, but I kept my face expressionless and just waited. "Try me."

"My father is alive."

I blinked and steadied myself. Had my son taken leave of his senses? "No, Jamie," I said calmly. "Your father is *not* alive. I saw him ... uh, in his coffin ... before the internment, and Hal was most assuredly—"

"No, not *that* father, Mom. William, I mean *Liam* O'Neil—he is alive."

"Jamie ..." I glanced toward the kitchen now, longing for someone to come out and help me make sense of this or at least bring some coffee to clear my head. "I think you must be confused—"

"No, Mom. I know it probably sounds crazy, and I had a feeling it would be hard for you to believe this. It wasn't easy for me either. But, really, I met him last night. Liam O'Neil is very much alive."

I considered this. "Do you mean you met someone by that name, because if that's the case, I'm sure there must be dozens of Liam O—"

"No, Mom, *really*, this is the guy—the real deal. We talked for a couple of hours. He told me everything—about Pearl Harbor, about you, and how he lost his leg."

I blinked and leaned back in my chair, trying to catch my breath and to take this in. Was Jamie crazy? "What on earth are you saying?"

"Liam O'Neil is alive. He's been living in Ireland for about fifteen years and he's a really great guy."

I felt like I couldn't breathe just now, like someone had wrapped a thick corset around my rib cage and pulled it tight. I wondered if I should lean over and put my head between my knees, allow some oxygen to my brain, but instead I just sat there, staring at my son. Was it possible that he'd been smoking some of that marijuana that I'd just read about? Or perhaps that other new drug LDS or SLD or whatever that mind-altering chemical was called?

"Jamie?" I tried again, my shaky voice coming out in a hoarse whisper. "Are you certain you weren't hallucinating?"

He actually smiled now. "Listen to me, I *really* met him. It was my piano music that brought this whole thing up. This lady named Margaret came up and told me that I played just like him, and she talked to me for a while, then introduced me to the guy, and it really was him." He was so excited that I couldn't help but almost believe him. "Isn't it great?"

I just shook my head, still trying to absorb all of this. Liam was alive . . . a woman named Margaret . . . they had spoken to my son. "And who is Margaret?" I finally asked. My voice sounded like that of a small child, and it felt as if the earth were moving beneath my feet, like I was losing my balance, tipping sideways.

"I don't really know exactly," he admitted. "I mean, she was with Liam and everything. But when she introduced herself, I think she said she was his friend." He brightened. "She's also a friend of Kerry's. Kerry introduced me to Margaret. And Liam and Margaret were with this other couple, I can't even remember their names, but they live near Clifden. Liam and Margaret live in Galway. I think they came to visit for the weekend."

I took in a shaky breath. "And what did Kerry think of all this? Was she convinced that this Liam person was really your father as well?"

"Of course. Because *he is*."

"But, Jamie . . . it just sounds so—so impossible."

So then he went into detail about how Liam had been on the SS *Arizona* when the bombs fell that day, and how he'd been seriously injured, unconscious for a long time, and how he lost a leg . . . and slowly it all began to sink in. It began to make a tiny speck of sense. Those were strange times back then. So much going on. I supposed people, papers, records . . . maybe it could've gotten mixed up.

"But what about the Red Cross?" I tried.

"Liam said he wasn't actually stationed in Honolulu," Jamie continued. "He was only supposed to be there for a couple of weeks. That's why they didn't have a record of him and probably why your letters were returned."

I nodded. Everything seemed fuzzy and blurry just now, as if the restaurant had filled with smoke, but no one was smoking. Although I wasn't a smoker, I almost felt as if I could use a cigarette. "Yes," I said meekly, "that sounds possible . . ."

"So, do you believe me now?"

"To be honest, I don't know what I think just now, Jamie." I glanced to the kitchen. "Could you see if someone could get me a cup of coffee . . . or a glass of water or something?" My throat felt tight and it was still difficult to breathe. I wasn't sure if I was about to cry or laugh or have a stroke. But Jamie left and came back after a couple of minutes with a cup of coffee.

I took a cautious sip, then a slow breath. "Thanks."

"Are you okay?"

"I don't know . . ."

"It was a shock. I understand. I wanted to tell you as carefully as possible."

"You did just fine, son." I took in another slow breath.

"It'll get better," he reassured me. "After it sinks in some. I was pretty stunned at first too."

I just nodded and took another sip of coffee. It was black and hot and I usually drank mine with cream, but right now I didn't care. Jamie waited patiently as I sat there slowly sipping my coffee in amazed silence. I felt like I wasn't really there just then, like I was just floating around and watching this woman and her son. Finally, I remembered the prayer I'd prayed in the stairs. I silently prayed it again. *God, help me with this.* That was all. I thought I could breathe again.

"Do you feel better now?" Jamie asked after I finished my coffee.

"Yes. I think so. But I suppose I'm still in shock. It's a lot to take in."

He reached over and put his hand on mine. "I know."

Then I smiled at my son. Despite my tumultuous feelings, I had to appreciate how mature he was being just now. How supportive and understanding. When had he grown up so fast? "Thanks."

We talked about it some more. Jamie told me how Margaret had mentioned how much he looked like Liam when he was younger. "She must've known him for a long time."

I nodded, almost afraid to admit it. "You do look like him, Jamie. Strikingly so."

"He seems really nice."

"Did he play piano for you?"

"No." Jamie frowned now. "But I'd sure like to hear him."

"That would be nice." Even as I said these words, I wondered at myself. How was I calmly sitting here? How was I able to hear all this without falling completely apart?

"You're going to see him too, aren't you?"

I considered this. "Do you think he wants to see me?"

"Of course!"

Finally the waitress appeared, refilled my coffee cup, and took our order. I didn't feel the least bit hungry, but I ordered a bowl of oatmeal anyway.

"I told him he could call today."

"Here?" I asked stupidly. "At the hotel?"

"Sure. Is that okay?"

My hand flew up to my hair. I knew I must look disheveled and how, feeling so rushed, I hadn't dressed very carefully, hadn't even put on lipstick. "When?"

"I don't know. Probably not this early."

"Yes, of course."

As I picked at my oatmeal, I wondered about Liam. What would he think of me now? I was so much older. And who was Margaret?

"Did Liam tell you if he married?" I asked suddenly. "Does he have children?"

"He didn't mention it."

"Oh . . ."

"How do you feel about him now, Mom?"

I stared at my son, looking so much like his father. "I don't know, Jamie. It's been so long that it doesn't even seem real to me. If I didn't have you, I might even doubt that I'd ever known someone named Liam O'Neil. It's like an old movie that I watched a long time ago."

"But it's real, Mom. He's real. You know that, right? You do believe me?"

"Yes, of course, I believe you." I looked down at the table. "Do you mind if I excuse myself, Jamie? I still need some time to process all this."

"Sure, Mom." He even stood as I got up. Such a gentleman. When had he grown up so nicely?

"I'll be in my room," I said as I set the linen napkin on the chair.

"I'll finish up my breakfast and then be in my room too."

Then, feeling slightly robotic, I mindlessly walked out of the dining room, mechanically up the stairs and into my room where I locked the door, then sat down on my still unmade bed and just cried. I wasn't sure exactly why I was crying—were they tears of regret? Fear? Anger? Relief? Or perhaps just a cleansing of sorts.

But, after the tears subsided, I knew I had only one resort. I knew that I needed to give all of this to God. It was far too much for me to carry alone. And so I did. Then I took a long, soothing bath, adding some salts that I'd picked up in town. After that, I carefully did my hair and my makeup. Then I put on the lovely black-and-white Donegal suit that I'd purchased in Dublin. I studied myself in the mirror, and although I was much older than the last time Liam had seen me, I thought perhaps I didn't look too bad.

I wasn't sure what to do then. I certainly didn't trust myself alone with my thoughts. If not for my prayers, I felt I was hanging by an emotional thread. So I went and knocked on Jamie's room and told him that I was going to take a walk.

"You won't be gone long, will you?" He looked worried.

"No, I just want to stretch my legs while the weather holds. I heard it's going to rain again this afternoon."

He grinned. "What a surprise."

"I may stop at McGinney's for a cup of coffee," I said. "And to read the paper."

He nodded as if making a mental note of this. "Okay."

Then I went for a little walk, but most of the shops were closed and the streets fairly deserted. Then I realized it was Sunday and people were probably at mass or church. Fortunately, McGinney's, as usual, was open. So I got my coffee and then sat and distracted myself by reading the paper. I'd been curious as to what was going on in the United States lately. Life had seemed tenuous since the Kennedy assassination, and I had meant to keep up on the news. I felt as if the future was shaky. Not just for me personally but for our whole country, perhaps the whole world.

"Colleen?"

I looked up from my paper and instantly knew who this tall handsome man was, but I was unable to answer.

"May I join you?"

I nodded and set the newspaper aside. "Liam?" The word emerged as a whisper.

He smiled as he sat. "Colleen, you look just as beautiful as ever."

I felt myself blushing. "You look fine too." I liked the distinctive gray hair that had gathered at his temples and the fine creases by his eyes, as if he smiled a lot. This made me feel happy.

"I'm still in complete shock." He slowly shook his head. "This is all so unbelievable."

"I know . . ."

"I have so many questions."

"So do I."

"Ladies first?"

I wasn't so sure I wanted to go first. I wasn't even sure where to begin. "I wrote to you in Honolulu," I finally said. "Over and over. My letters were all returned."

"That's what Jamie said."

"I was frantic when I discovered I was pregnant." I shook my head as I recalled the horror at that discovery.

"I wish we'd gotten married."

"I was so stupid."

"You were trying to be sensible."

"No," I admitted. "I was being selfish and vain. I wanted to have a real *wedding*. I wanted my family to come out and meet you. I wanted to show you off." I looked down at the table, swallowed hard against the lump in my throat.

"I *tried* to find you, Colleen. I really did."

"Jamie told me that."

"When I got back to the mainland, you and Wanda weren't at the apartment. No one knew where either of you had gone, there was no forwarding address. I made so many phone calls to Johnson families in Southern California, all with no results . . . finally I just gave up. It seemed like you had vanished into thin air."

"We lost the apartment. Wanda got married, her name changed. And my family is just one of thousands of Johnsons in Minnesota, not California." I sighed at the hopelessness of two people separated by war and life and death and desperate circumstances. "I got a job selling shoes . . . I moved to Pasadena in December, then got married after a couple of months . . . my last name changed to Frederick."

"Jamie told me that your husband died a year and a half ago."

"Hal was a good man, he took good care of us."

He nodded sadly. "Did you love him?"

"I was desperate . . . I didn't think I could raise a child by myself. Hal loved me and in time I learned to love him . . . in a way . . . and he was a good dad to Jamie."

"Jamie is a fine young man. You did an excellent job raising him."

This made me laugh. "Jamie is what Jamie was going to be. I think you've had as much to do with it as I have—he is so like you."

He seemed to consider this. "I just couldn't believe it when I heard him playing the piano last night." Liam's eyes lit up. "It was so amazing to find out who he was. I'm sure my friends thought I was about to have a heart attack. I never dreamed I had a son, Colleen—that we had a son. It was so incredible, surreal. But hearing him on the piano, well, I just *knew*."

"I sort of know what you mean about the piano." Then I told him about my own experience less than a week ago, how Jamie had taken me so by surprise and how I had only told him the truth about Liam after that. "That's why I brought him to Ireland," I explained. "I thought it was the perfect place to tell him."

"More perfect than you knew."

Liam's eyes seemed to look right into me—past my calm veneer and straight to my soul. I wasn't sure what to say now. "I'm curious about your friends," I finally ventured. "Jamie mentioned them to me."

"Devin and I have been friends for years. He and Myrna have a lovely home a bit outside of Clifden. We came out here for the weekend—a little getaway. And Margaret is an old friend of mine."

I nodded as if that was all very nice, but I really wanted to ask him more about Margaret. What kind of "old friend" was she?

"Did Jamie tell you about my leg?" He held up his cane as if it were a prop. "Lost it in Pearl Harbor."

"Yes. I was so sorry to hear that. That must've been hard."

"Not nearly as hard as losing you. . ." Was there a trace of bitterness in his voice? Was it about me or the leg?

"I'm so sorry, Liam."

"I eventually resolved myself to my unlucky lot in life. It could've been worse . . . so many didn't survive that day. I finally convinced myself it might've been for the best—not finding you, I mean. I wasn't sure how you'd react to a one-legged husband, and I wasn't sure how I'd react to being rejected."

"And I might've been married by the time you found me," I said, which was sad but true.

He looked down at the table, tracing a long, graceful forefinger over the grain of the wood.

"So, did you marry, Liam? Have children?"

"No to both."

"I'm sorry."

His eyes twinkled now. "Wait. I take that back. I *did* have a child."

"Oh, yes!" My hand flew up to my mouth to think of this. "Jamie."

He leaned forward eagerly. "I want to get to know him better."

"I don't know why you shouldn't."

"He said you were going back to the States after the holidays."

"Our tickets are for the twenty-sixth," I admitted. "Jamie had insisted we keep the trip to two weeks. He wanted to be home for New Year's Eve."

"Big plans, eh?"

I shrugged. I still wanted to ask him more about this Margaret person. But how did one do this gracefully? At least they weren't married. That was some consolation. But what if they were involved? Besides, it was quite possible that Liam had no feelings left for me. After all, I was the one who gave up so quickly. I was the one who got married.

We continued to talk, filling in some of the blank spaces, telling each other bits and pieces of so much that had happened in the past twenty-two years. I told him a lot about Jamie. And he told me about how returning to Ireland was a life-changing experience for him, explaining how he found himself as well as God here on the Emerald Isle. It was quite a moving story. I even told him about how I'd been learning to let go of my hold on Jamie and trusting God instead. Perhaps it had to do with Ireland.

And to my surprise, after an hour or so, I felt fairly relaxed—almost as if we hadn't been apart all those years. It was amazing, really. And I loved hearing about Liam's life. How he'd returned to college on his GI bill and gotten his music degree, how he'd taught at several universities and occasionally did concerts here in Ireland. "Music is an enormous part of my life."

"How exciting," I said, marveling again at the color of his eyes—still as intensely blue as ever. "Does Jamie know about any of this?"

"We didn't get terribly far last night. To be honest, I was so stunned that I hardly recall what we did speak about."

"He'll be thrilled to get to know you. He loves music dearly, more so than I even knew, and I'm afraid I haven't been terribly encouraging."

"This is all so incredible," he said suddenly. "I feel as if I should pinch myself. To think I have a real son—a talented son who appreciates music as much as I do." His eyes got misty now. "It's such a fantastic gift! What a grand Christmas this will be!"

Of course, I was thrilled that he was so excited about Jamie. But I wanted to ask him where I fit into this picture. I knew it was unrealistic to assume we could pick up right where we left off. But how did he really feel about me? Was it too late for us? And what about Margaret? What was she to him? But it was as if these questions were bottled up tight, the cork jammed down. I couldn't get a single one out.

"I'm sure you guessed that Jamie was the one who told me where to find you this morning." Liam looked at his watch. "And I told him that I'd love to spend some time with him before we have to head back to Galway. Margaret has a function there at two this afternoon, so our time today is limited."

"Oh . . ."

He reached for my hand and gave it a warm squeeze. "It's been so great seeing you, Colleen. Really amazing."

I nodded, forcing a bright smile as I held back tears. "You too, Liam."

"Are you going back to the hotel now? Shall we walk together?"

I glanced at the paper still at my elbow. "I think I'll stay here a little longer," I said in a restrained voice. "I, uh, I think I'll get another cup of coffee and finish the newspaper first."

He nodded and stood. "Take care now."

"You too." Then as soon as he was out the door, I picked up the newspaper, and using it like a privacy screen, I started to cry.

16

Jamie

I knew this Christmas was going to be the best ever! For one thing, we were in Ireland and that was pretty amazing in itself. But besides that, I was going to spend the holidays with Liam, my biological father. Before leaving Clifden on Sunday, Liam had invited me to come to Galway for the holidays. Of course, he extended the invitation to my mom as well. But since he had to get back to Galway and Mom wasn't around, he asked me to ask her for him. Even so, I could tell he wanted her to come.

"You just missed Liam," I told Mom as she came into the hotel lobby.

"Actually I saw him being picked up in front just now."

"Did you talk to him?"

"Well, no . . . but I saw him getting into a nice Mercedes Benz with a pretty blonde woman at the wheel."

I smiled. "Yeah, that was Margaret. Did you know that she's a musician too?"

"No, I didn't."

"Yeah," I told her. "Liam said that she plays several instruments—they both do. And they're having this huge Christmas Eve party with all their musical friends. And everyone will be playing music and Liam invited me to join them. He said I can play the piano or borrow his guitar or whatever. Isn't that cool?"

"I'm sure you'll have a good time, Jamie."

"But you're coming too," I said quickly. "Liam said I could invite you."

"That was nice of him." Mom sighed as if she was bored, or perhaps it was something more.

"You do want to come, don't you?"

"Oh, I don't know . . ."

"Come on, Mom. It's going to be great. You have to come to Galway. After all, it's going to be Christmas." I knew how Mom felt about the holidays. Family was supposed to be together. I'd broken that cardinal rule last year, and I didn't intend to repeat that same mistake.

Her brow creased and I was afraid she was about to say no.

"Is it because of Liam?" I asked suddenly. "Are you uncomfortable with him?"

"It's hard to explain . . . I'm not even sure how I feel. Or how he feels . . ."

"Even more reason to come," I urged. "Liam seemed like he really wanted you there in Galway. You've got to come."

She smiled. "Okay, Jamie, I'll come to Galway with you." She glanced over to the front desk. "That is if I can get it all arranged. It's awfully late notice and it's the holidays. We might not be able to find accommodations."

"I already asked the concierge to do some calling for us."

She looked surprised at my assertiveness. Then she smiled and I knew it would be okay. As it turned out, the concierge knew just the place, and by the end of the day, it was all set.

So it was that on Christmas Eve day, following a leisurely lunch with Kerry and Dolan at the Anchor Inn, we checked out of our Clifden hotel and a hired car took us to Galway, where we checked into a very posh hotel right in the center of town.

"Merry Christmas, son," she said as she handed me a key to my room. "I hope this is really what you wanted."

I hugged her. "It's perfect. Thanks so much. Liam said to come over anytime after six. It's not a sit-down dinner, but they'll have plenty of food."

"Oh, I don't know that I'll go to the party," she said in a tired tone. "I'm feeling a little worn out and—"

"You have to come. It won't feel like Christmas without you."

"I don't know . . ."

"Come on," I persisted. "It's only one night. And we'll be going back home in just two days. You need to make the most of it."

"I suppose you're right. But I can't be ready by six. You can head on over there ahead of me if you like—"

"Not a chance," I told her. "I'll wait and go with you."

She looked slightly relieved. "Okay. Then I plan to take a nice, long bath first. And I won't be ready to leave until seven."

I grinned. "That's fine. I'll meet you in the lobby, okay?"

She frowned slightly, then nodded. I wasn't completely sure why Mom was having such a hard time with this. Was it because of her old relationship with Liam? Was she feeling nervous about where things stood with them now? Of course, that made some sense, but it had been such a long time ago that they'd been involved. Still, it seemed possible she could still have feelings for him. Although she hadn't said anything to make me think this. If anything, she'd been pretty tight-lipped about the whole thing. Well, other than asking about Margaret. She had tried to sound disinterested and casual, but I could tell she was concerned that Margaret and Liam were involved. To be honest, I wasn't sure. They did seem to be pretty good friends.

As I went into my room, I wondered what it would be like to be Mom's age and suddenly have an old flame popping back into my life. I suppose if it was Shelly, telling me she'd made a mistake and that she wanted me back, well, I'd probably stand up and take notice. Still, it'd be awkward. I had to admit that much. But if nothing else, I hoped that Liam and Mom could be friends. What kid wouldn't want that much from his parents?

Mom was a few minutes late, but when she came into the lobby, I felt proud to think that this lady was my mother. She had on a dark red velvet dress that looked fantastic. She even had the mink stole that my dad had gotten her for Christmas a few years ago. And as we waited for our taxi, a gentleman going into the hotel really checked her out and even tipped his hat.

"You look like a million bucks," I told her.

She thanked me and we got into the back of the taxi.

"Since this side trip to Galway is your Christmas present to me," I began as I pulled a small bundle from my pocket, "I thought I should give my present to you too."

She smiled and looked curious. "You really got me something?"

I nodded and unwrapped the tissue paper to expose a small silver ring that I'd bought in Clifden. It was shaped like two hands holding a heart. "It's a traditional Irish ring," I explained.

"A Claddagh?" she said with excitement.

"Yes," I said, suddenly remembering the name.

"Oh, I had wanted to get one."

"It's only silver," I said. "And the lady at the shop said that you're supposed to wear it on your right hand with the heart pointing away from your fingers."

"Really?" She slipped the ring on. "It fits! How did you know?"

I grinned. "Just lucky, I guess."

Then Mom hugged me. "Thank you, Jamie. I will treasure this always."

We were out of the city and driving through a neighborhood now, probably getting close to the place. And I could tell by the way Mom started twisting the handle on her little black evening purse that she was getting nervous. I hoped I wouldn't be sorry that I'd talked her into coming tonight. I was starting to feel worried about the status of Liam's relationship with Margaret. Even though Margaret was older, probably in her late thirties, I had to admit she was really good-looking. I glanced at Mom and mentally compared the two women. While Margaret was pretty in that flashy blonde sort of way, I thought my mom had a very classic sort of beauty.

"Liam said they play a lot of traditional Irish folk music," I said for no apparent reason, except that I was hoping to fill in the dead silence of the taxi. "It's supposed to be like an old-fashioned Irish Christmas." I said a few more random things, but I suspect that Mom knew I was trying too hard. And I was probably just making both of us even more nervous.

Liam's house was on the outskirts of town. Situated in an impressive-looking neighborhood, it was a large stone house with lots of tall windows. Each window had a candle burning in it—I'd heard that was an Irish Christmas tradition—but it gave the house an inviting appearance. There was a huge holly wreath on the shiny red door, and we'd barely rung the bell when it was opened wide and we were welcomed by the happy sound of music.

"Come in," said a man in a dark suit as he held the door and took our coats, pointing us in the direction of the music.

I spotted Liam immediately. He was playing the fiddle along with several other musicians on other traditional Irish instruments, including Margaret, who was playing a lively piece on the mandolin. Margaret stood right next to Liam, looking up into his face with an expression that seemed to convey more than just a casual musician friendship, although I hoped I was wrong. I glanced at Mom in time to see her nervously fingering the strand of white pearls that circled her neck. It was possible that this evening was going to turn into a great big mistake. As badly as I wanted to participate in the music and all, I hated to think that I was ruining Mom's Christmas.

"Want to sit down?" I asked, pointing to a comfortable-looking chair near the fireplace. "I can get you something to drink or some food or something."

"Something to drink would be nice." She spoke to me, but her eyes were on the mandolin player. And it was hard not to stare at Margaret since she had on this silver sequined dress that was cut low in the front, and showing a fair amount of leg as well. Mom sat down and I went off in search of something to drink just as the song ended.

"I didn't see you come in," Liam said when he joined me at the large cut crystal punch bowl. "Is your mother here too?"

I nodded. "I was just getting her something to drink."

"This is a traditional Irish Christmas punch," he told me. "It's Margaret's special recipe, but I should warn you it has a bit of rum in it."

I considered this. Mom wasn't much of a drinker. But perhaps this wasn't a bad idea tonight. Maybe it would help her to relax. "That was a great song you guys just played," I said as I filled a cup.

"Do you want to join us on the next number? Are you good at improvisation?"

"I'd like to give it a try."

He grinned at me, then nodded toward a large table with an assortment of musical instruments arranged upon it. "Pick your instrument and come on up."

I took Mom her punch, then excused myself to join Liam and his friends.

"Don't worry about me," she assured me. "I'm perfectly fine, Jamie. You go and have fun. It'll be a delight just to listen."

I still felt a little guilty, but appreciated her attitude. This was such a great opportunity—a once-in-a-lifetime Christmas. I chose the guitar and joined the others, and before long I was picking and strumming to a lively Irish folk tune. It felt so natural to play like this, like it really was something in my blood. It seemed to be the same sort of feeling that I'd been putting into my piano playing this past year. But I could never quite figure it out or even put a name to it. Now I wondered if it was simply "Irish." I didn't know how many songs I'd played with the others before I remembered my mom. I hoped she didn't feel abandoned.

"How are you doing?" I asked as I joined her again.

She smiled happily. "I'm absolutely fine, Jamie. And the music is lovely. Please, don't feel that you need to entertain your poor old mother."

I laughed. "There's nothing poor or old about you."

She smiled at a gray-haired woman sitting to her right. "And I've made a new friend tonight." Then she introduced me to Mrs. Flanders. "She's Liam's neighbor and an artist. We've been having a great time getting acquainted."

"And you are a talented lad," Mrs. Flanders said. "I nearly fell over when Liam informed me that he had a son joining us tonight." She shook her head. "Remarkable!"

Mom smiled at Mrs. Flanders, but her eyes seemed a little sad. "So, really, Jamie, please, don't worry about me. Just enjoy this evening. I love watching you play. I had no idea you were this good."

"I take after my father." I winked at her.

"You sure do." Her smile looked genuine now. "And I'm so proud of you!"

So, feeling relieved that Mom at least had someone to chat with, I returned to the musicians, and this time, seeing that no one was at the piano, I slipped in and began to play along. Liam grinned at me as he picked up the discarded guitar and surprised me with some very tricky fretwork. This guy could teach me a lot!

As the evening wore on, we began to play more Christmas music and some of the less musical spectators even started to sing along with us. Margaret was a pro at getting the crowd enthused. She'd shout out the words and they'd join in. It was such a happy evening and such a great mix of people. Not to mention that the music was amazing. And, for the first time that I can ever recall, I felt as if I completely fit in. It was better than when I'd led Jamie and the Muskrats and better than when I'd met the Irish musicians in Dublin and wished I could join their band.

This was unlike anything I'd ever experienced before. It felt as if I'd finally come home. I was so comfortable here, playing with my biological father and his musician friends, that it was indescribably cool. Extremely groovy. The only disappointing part of the evening, and something that seemed completely out of my control, was the aura of sadness that seemed to drape itself around my mother. Oh, she was smiling and clapping and even singing along when she knew the words. But her eyes . . . they were full of sadness. And I feared this was probably the longest evening of her life—and she was doing it for me. And, despite my guilt, it was so hard to quit playing. But when I checked on her, she reassured me that she was having a good time. And so I was back on the guitar again, and as we played and played, I honestly thought I could carry on like this for hours. Maybe even days.

Finally it was nearing midnight and the crowd was still going strong, but I noticed that Liam had taken a break. And so I decided this was a good time for me to call it a night. I didn't want to leave, but I knew Mom had made her sacrifice in coming here tonight. I could make mine by leaving early.

But when I went to look for her, she wasn't in the chair. Neither was Mrs. Flanders. Maybe they'd gone off together, although that seemed unlikely. So I got a bite to eat, then looked around for Mom, but didn't see her anywhere. Had she called a taxi and gone back to the hotel by herself? And, if so, why didn't she let me know? I decided to see if I could find Liam, perhaps I could use his phone to call the hotel. But I didn't see him anywhere either. Finally I spotted Margaret, adding some more rum to the punch.

"Have you seen Liam?" I asked.

She glanced around. "No, but he might be in the library. He sometimes takes a break in there." She pointed to a hallway near the stairs. "Second door to the left."

I thanked her and headed in that direction, pausing by what I thought was the door to the library. Other than a slit, it was mostly closed, but I could hear voices talking quietly—male and female. I strained my ears to hear better, unsure as to whether I wanted to interrupt or not, when I realized it was Liam talking to my mother. I couldn't quite make out the words, but there was a sound of urgency in Liam's tone. And it almost sounded as if my mother was crying, which worried me.

I actually leaned over now and, feeling like a snoop or maybe just a kid trying to sneak a peek at Santa, I peered through the crack just in time to see Liam taking my mother into his arms—and she was not resisting—and kissing her with such force and passion that I had to look away. There was only so much that a son wants to know about his mother's love life. Besides I knew this was a private moment.

But I retreated back to the kitchen feeling just slightly victorious. Of course, this didn't really make sense. But somehow I felt just a little responsible for reuniting my two parents like this. If it hadn't been for me, Mom never would've come to Ireland. If we hadn't come to Ireland, we never would've met Liam.

"Did you find Liam?" Margaret asked as I returned to the punch bowl.

"Yeah." I studied her for a moment, wondering how she was going to take this new development.

"Were they together?" she asked as she ladled out some punch. "I mean your mother and Liam?"

I blinked. "You know?"

She shrugged. "I've known for years, Jamie."

"Seriously?"

She took a sip of punch, then nodded.

"How did you know?"

"For starters, I'd have to swear you to secrecy."

I held up my fingers in the old pledge. "Scout's honor."

"Can I really trust you?"

"Yes," I urged. "Now tell me what it is that you've known for years."

She let out a big sigh. "That if Colleen ever walked back into Liam's life . . . well, let me just say that I've always known that he never quit loving her."

"And you're okay with that?"

She nodded with misty eyes. "Liam is a very good friend. How could I not be happy for him? Colleen was the love of his life and he thought he'd lost her forever." Then she threw her arms around me. "And you, young man, are one of the most amazing young musicians that I've had the pleasure to meet. Has your father talked to you about attending university here in Galway yet?"

"Not yet."

"Well, he should!"

17

Colleen

On the day after Christmas, also Saint Stephen's Day and an Irish holiday, I stood in the relatively quiet Dublin airport by myself. I felt surprisingly torn about leaving Ireland. But I felt even more torn that I was leaving my son behind. Of course, I was glad that he wanted to finish college, even if it was in Galway, halfway around the globe from our home in Pasadena. And I'd been especially touched when he told me that he also planned to get a job. "I want to pay you back for what I wasted on my phony education," he told me over breakfast yesterday. Now my first instinct had been to say no and that the debt was forgiven and not to worry about it, but on second thought, I wondered if this was something he needed to do—another step in becoming a man and a responsible adult. So I bit my tongue and hid my motherly pride.

But I missed Jamie more than ever just now as I waited to board my plane. The idea of going home—alone like this—was overwhelming and nothing I had ever imagined when I started this trip, oh, a lifetime ago. Still, I reminded myself, it was time for me to accept my independence. I didn't need anyone to hold my hand. I was a grown woman and perfectly capable of carrying my own bags, sitting on a plane by myself, catching a taxi back to the house, making plans for my future . . . even if that meant I would be the only one in the picture. And, after all, I did have God to lean on. I wasn't really alone.

"But what about Liam?" Jamie had demanded in my room just last night, right after I'd informed him of my plans to go home on the regularly scheduled flight. For some reason he'd gotten the idea that, like him, I planned to extend my visit.

"What about Liam?" I had calmly asked as I carefully packed my bags.

"He loves you," he said. "Don't you love him?"

I smiled patiently at my son. I knew he meant well. "This really isn't your problem, Jamie."

"But I saw you kissing on Christmas Eve," he confessed.

I blinked back surprise. "You were spying on us?"

He nodded sheepishly. "Sort of. I mean I hadn't meant to, but I did see you two together. And it looked pretty obvious that you were both in love."

"I'd had too much of that Irish punch," I told him. "I was impaired."

"That wasn't the case, Mom."

"Jamie, I know it's every child's hope that his parents would be in love and stay in love and that everyone would live happily ever after, but it can't always be like that."

"But Liam *does* love you."

I studied Jamie closely. "How do you know that? Has he told you that?"

"No, he hasn't said that, not in so many words. But I know it's true. I have my reasons to believe it's true. You have to trust me on this, Mom."

I turned my attention to the folding of my red velvet dress, the same dress I'd been wearing that night. And I had to admit that I had felt that way too. I had honestly believed that Liam did still love me—especially on Christmas Eve, when we had kissed. But he had never *said* so. Consequently, I hadn't told him how I felt either. Although it seemed obvious that night—to me anyway. But then Jamie and I had left. And then there was the next day. And there was Margaret.

On Christmas Day, when we got together with Liam and some of his friends again, he privately admitted to me that Margaret had been in his life for years—and even that she had recently been pushing him toward marriage. He seemed very confused and uncomfortable with all this. He didn't say it, but I felt that I was an interruption, a distraction, and an inconvenience. And, after all, Liam had known Margaret much longer than he'd known me—they'd spent years and years together. Simply because Liam and I had made a son together didn't mean that we were meant to be together. And then I'd seen how compatible he and Margaret appeared to be—so much in common with their music, their lives, and Ireland. And she was so beautiful. How was I supposed to compete with that?

"You can't leave, Mom."

"I'm sorry." I turned and faced him with a firm chin. "But I have to go home. For one thing, I have the house on the market, and the last time I spoke to the realtor, right before Christmas, she thought she had a buyer for it."

"Great," he said. "Sell the house. But why do you have to go home to do that?"

"It's the mature and responsible thing to do," I explained as I rolled a pair of stockings.

And so, as I stood there so carefully dressed in my Donegal suit with matching shoes and handbag, waiting for my flight to begin loading, I thought I was being remarkably responsible and mature. Or at least I looked that way. Despite how I felt inside, I wasn't crying or fretting or fuming or any other childish thing. I was simply waiting to get on my plane and go home. And, once I got home, I would begin to sort out my life again. Perhaps the house would be sold by then. Maybe I would find that little cottage near the beach after all. And who knew, I might even get a job. The possibilities were endless.

"Colleen?"

I didn't turn at the sound of his voice. Not immediately, anyway. But my stomach grew fluttery and there was a catch in my throat as I slowly pivoted and faced him.

"Liam." I studied his eyes, trying to read what was behind them. "What are you doing here? Is something wrong? Is it Jamie?"

He took a tentative step toward me. "Jamie is fine."

"Oh . . ."

"It's Jamie's father who is having trouble."

"Jamie's father?"

"Yes, Colleen. I am perfectly miserable."

"Oh . . ."

"I can't let you go like this."

"Like what?"

"I can't let you go without telling you the truth first."

I nodded now, bracing myself for the worst. Perhaps he and Margaret had gotten engaged last night, after Jamie and I had left. Perhaps Liam felt that the mature thing for him to do was to come here and tell me this news in person. Maybe Jamie had said something to make Liam think that I would need to know. "Yes?" I heard my voice shaking.

"I love you, Colleen."

I blinked, then stared, unable to speak. Had I heard him correctly?

"I never quit loving you."

"But why didn't you say something . . ."

He held out his cane. "I don't like to talk about it, Colleen. It's hard to admit . . . but being a man with one leg, well, it's not been easy. To be honest, it's probably one of the main reasons I never asked Margaret to marry."

I sucked in a quick breath. "So, you would've asked her?"

He nodded then sighed. "Yes. I probably would've."

"Why don't you ask her now?"

"Because I don't *love* her. Not like this."

"Oh . . ."

"I love *you*, Colleen." He peered at me with those intense blue eyes. "And are you going to just hang me out to dry now? Do you have nothing to say?"

I took a step toward him, our eyes still locked. "I love you too, Liam. I always have. I always will. I never quit loving you."

Then he took me into his arms and held me tight. "Please, don't go."

"But I need to take care of things back home," I began meekly. But suddenly he was kissing me, his lips pressed into mine with passion and intensity—the kind I had longed for since that November of 1941. And in that moment I felt both lost and found, and without holding back, I returned his kiss.

"Please, don't go," he said again. "Stay here and marry me, Colleen."

I almost said no, not now. I almost told him that I needed to go back to Pasadena and that I needed to take care of business—that I needed to be a grown-up and to sell my house, that I needed to store my furniture, that I needed to tell my sister the good news, and I almost told him that we should wait—but I stopped myself.

"Yes!" I said with excitement. "I *will* stay here and I *will* marry you!"

His brows shot up with surprise. "You will? You really will?"

"Of course! You don't think I'm going to make the same mistake twice, do you? I'm not taking any chances this time. *Yes, I will marry you!*"

Then he took my right hand in his and carefully removed the silver ring that Jamie had given me for Christmas.

"What?" I frowned and felt slightly worried.

"Now you must wear the Claddagh like this." He took my left hand and slipped the ring onto my ring finger with the point of the heart aiming toward me. "Worn like this means your heart is taken."

I nodded. "You took it long ago, Liam."

"Let's go get married!" he said as he pulled me close for another long kiss.

"You just name the day and the time, and I will gladly marry you, Liam O'Neil."

"Let's go round up a preacher." He grinned down at me. "And I know a certain young man—a man who's waiting outside in my car right this minute—who will be extremely happy to hear about this."

I grabbed Liam's hand. "Let's go tell him!"

Melody Carlson is the prolific author of more than 200 books, including fiction, nonfiction, and gift books for adults, young adults, and children. She is also the author of *Three Days, The Gift of Christmas Present,* and *The Christmas Bus.* Her writing has won several awards, including a Gold Medallion for *King of the Stable* (Crossway, 1998) and a Romance Writers of America Rita Award for *Homeward* (Multnomah, 1997). She lives with her husband in Sisters, Oregon. Visit her website at www.melodycarlson.com.